JOHN PENNINGTON was born in Cheshire in 1939 and still lives there in a small village in the heart of the county. It is an area known for the training of racehorses. For five years, he lived and worked opposite a trainer's yard and assimilated the daily routine unconsciously. He has written for radio and television for many years. His long list of credits has included highly successful series such as *Coronation Street, The Mask of Janus, Dr Finlay's Casebook, The Expert* and *The Brothers*. His first radio play, called *The Tin on the Wall*, was about life in a bookmaker's office. He feels that he has come full circle by currently writing for the BBC drama series *Trainer*.

He is married to the artist Bernadette Pennington and they have a daughter, Fiona, who is a Cambridge history graduate.

JOHN PENNINGTON

TRAINER

A Pan Original
PAN BOOKS
LONDON, SYDNEY AND AUCKLAND

A Pan Original

First published in Great Britain 1991 by
Pan Books Ltd, Cavaye Place, London SW10 9PG

1 3 5 7 9 9 8 6 4 2

© John Pennington 1991

ISBN 0 330 32360 1

Typeset by Intype, London
Printed in England by Clays Ltd, St Ives plc

ACKNOWLEDGEMENTS

Trainer, the BBC Television series, is devised by Gerard
Glaister and Tony Lakin, and produced by Gerard Glaister.
The Story Consultant is Christopher Green and the Script
Editor is Colin Brake. The writers are Christopher Green,
John Pennington, Brian Finch, Colin Blumeau, Gawn
Grainger and Tony Jordan, and the series is directed by
Jeremy Summers, Frank Smith and Tristan de Vere Cole.

To Bernadette and Fiona

FOREWORD

This book is loosely based on the BBC television drama series *TRAINER*, shot entirely on film.

I have not seen the footage. Nor have I sought to transcribe the scripts into prose, because the two forms are so different. Often, what can be seen cannot be said. Equally, what can be thought cannot be seen.

What is written here will not necessarily appear on the screen, either in story-line or dialogue.

But in passing, I have tried to paint in broad fashion some of the background of the world of horse racing, for readers who have no knowledge of it.

To those who are more than familiar, I offer my apologies for errors not allowed by the slim defence of dramatic licence.

I have been overwhelmed by the kindness and attention to detail shown during my twelve-month research by the remarkable men and women who are daily engaged in 'The Sport of Kings'. They have answered my many questions with tolerance and wry good humour.

Amongst them have been trainers, jockeys, bookmakers, tic-tacs, starters, clerks of the scales, judges, stewards, stable lads, owners, veterinarians, valets, breeders and, of course, gamblers – the punters without whom the whole industry would collapse.

There are vivid memories of being privileged to sit in

the Weighing Room, or beside the Judge in his box. I have stood behind hastily erected canvas screens at a racecourse, as the vet put his gun to the head of a magnificent beast with a shattered pastern. And in the dark hours of the night, I have assisted with the birth of a foal.

I should mention my thanks to Ted Greenway, the vet who has devoted his life to horses, and Terry Caldwell, a trainer who has given me much of his time, Ray Peacock, David Norcliffe who trades as a racecourse bookmaker under the name of David Hudson, for his unflagging corrections, Celia Radband, the talented lady jockey, and Peter Cundell, the series adviser, for his many kindnesses.

But there would be a long list if I gave the names of everyone who assisted in revealing to me a little of the glorious world of racing.

John Pennington

ONE

The newly painted wooden board read:

ARKENFIELD STABLES
Trainer: Michael Hardy
Arkenfield, Berkshire

Mike surveyed it from across the lane, partly hidden by the hedge. For him, the hour after evening stables was the worst of the day. Above the red-brick Victorian buildings and slate roof-tops, against the early April rainclouds, the weather-vane, shaped like a galloping racehorse, shifted in the wind.

One good horse. All I need is one good horse, he thought.

It would introduce his name and methods to the world of flat racing. It would lead to another good horse. Then a stable filled with good horses, not the rags he had now. He would pick his owners. He would not have to smile and be grateful to ignorant millionaires like James Brant, who had backed him and bought the once-derelict yard.

But he was grateful.

James Brant had changed his life. His motive may have been self-serving, but Mike had grabbed at the chance. Brant was paying less for his training now than he had when his horses were at Latimer's. He wasn't really his own boss. But his name was up there on the board.

He wanted everyone to see it.

His father had been Head Lad at Latimer's before him. Drink and grief had made an old man of him in his fifties. Early retirement, unheeded medical warnings and a build-up of blood pressure led to a series of strokes which finished him off four years ago. Mike shared the grief, which was caused by the death of his mother in a road accident.

That was in 1976, in his last week of school.

Would his mother and father be proud of him now? He doubted it.

His elder sister, Ruth, who hated horses and talk of horses, emigrated to Australia with a freckled-faced young man. She was happy, the occasional card said.

As a family, Mike often thought, they were as dumb as horses. Mike's father rarely spoke, while his mother chattered, but said nothing. Words were a problem for Mike. He found himself not saying what he meant, or blurting words out wrongly, causing offence. Words on paper were worse. He hardly wrote letters because he was ashamed of them, and they took him hours to compose.

Words were needed now because so much of the job of a trainer was talking to owners. They wanted to know why their horses were beaten, why they were sick, why the going was wrong, why the jockey failed. Training owners was more difficult than training racehorses.

Sally had been good with words. But when she left, after three years of marriage and a lot of words, she walked out with their son, Tom, without even saying goodbye. Wrangles with lawyers produced pages of costly words. They didn't come back.

She emigrated to Australia, too, with an Irish jockey full of blarney, on his way to stardom.

The pain hadn't lessened. It struck every morning when

8

he woke up at six and lingered through the day until that hour after evening stables, when whisky would deaden it a little. Whisky – whisky and beer – and more whisky, to smother it. Until it came alive again in his dreams.

But he had not drunk whisky or beer for months, not since they began refurbishing the yard.

James Brant had been clear about that. He had no room for a man with a drink problem.

Was Mike an alcoholic?

The pain was still there. There was no relief from it, except when he was working. He saw his son's face everywhere. What would he look like now? Tom Fisher, the solicitor, had negotiated access, while talking about horses. Mike could visit his son any weekend he liked, in New South Wales.

Rain glistened on the slates and spotted his pale fawn jodhpurs. He moved away from the hedge and strode across the lane towards the wire-mesh security gates of Arkenfield.

He needed a whisky now.

Picking a good horse is easy after the event. Whatever the size, colour, sex, age, breeding or conformation – a good horse is first past the post in a good race. Picking it beforehand is hard.

The thoroughbred is the fastest horse in the world. All of them, without exception, trace back to three famous stallions in England, the home of horse racing, in the early eighteenth century. The first of these founding fathers was the charger of the English Captain Byerley at the Battle of the Boyne in 1690.

The Byerley Turk, the Darley Arabian and the Godol-

9

phin Arabian and their thousands of progeny, raised only one question.

Will the horse win?

It's a question that hovers in the minds of everyone in racing. From the beginning of the covering season in the middle of February, when the best stallions are put to the best mares, to the birth, eleven months later, of astonishing foals, standing in minutes and galloping in days, all eyes look and question. From the awkward yearlings in the Sales, to the breaking in the trainer's yard, the early schooling, building muscle and bone, gathering speed, they ask the unanswerable. Nobody knows.

A lad on the back of a horse in training, riding the gallops soon after dawn, may have an idea. A student of form, considering going, fitness, class and conditions, makes a guess. But nobody knows for sure. That is the endless fascination of racing.

Many horses never win. Thousands of them occupy stables, eating well, with high hopes, training daily. Flying their owner's colours, they gallop madly for a few minutes on race days, with keen jockeys on their backs, and they are tailed off, going backwards, beaten a bus ride.

James Brant owned eight useless horses. But he had no idea of that. Hugo Latimer, his previous trainer, had been well paid for finding and buying them. Money talked, Brant knew, and he was confident that soon he would stand in the Winner's Enclosure, perhaps at Royal Ascot. He would smile modestly, his back-street origins forgotten, and meet, who knew – the Queen?

Then his worth would be recognized.

Brant was a fighter who left school at fifteen, glad to escape. Smashing the nose of a bully was his only achievement there. He went straight into the building trade as an apprentice plasterer, and switched to bricklaying after a brawl which had someone in hospital. Bored, he went to night school to learn to be an electrician.

National Service taught him to hate officers. They had power of another sort. He decided that he had to be his own boss, in civilian life.

After leaving the army, he bought an ash tip from the Council for a nominal sum and sold the ash to the building trade in lorry loads, making big profits. Then he bought streets and demolished them, bulldozing acres of the sort of back-to-back houses he grew up in.

He married young. Kath was a grammar school girl, in her final year at university, who represented the education he felt he lacked. They were content with each other. Only their childlessness caused pain, but neither had the nerve to investigate the reason.

Then he began building . . .

Through his office window Mike watched the rain lashing the circular wooden tack-room in the centre of the yard.

Whisky and water would drown the feeling crawling in his stomach. All he wanted was to be in the Dog and Gun where the lads were enjoying themselves, sinking pints in the favoured early-doors session. Jokes, racing-talk and village gossip.

Gossip branded Mike a drunk and a failure. The first months after Sally walked out, he had lived in that pub. Drunk and loosened, he poured out his pain to anyone, seeking consolation, self-justification, sympathy. For a man of few words, he had said far too much.

David Ware listened and used it against him.

An American in his mid-twenties, educated at Harvard

11

without a degree, spoiled by his mother, attractive and devilish. Mike mistook his charm for concern.

David Ware's father, Frank, owned farms in Kentucky and the Ware Stud in Arkenfield. Frank was dead now. But six months before he died, he saw sense. His life had been breeding and bloodstock on both sides of the Atlantic. He finally recognized that his only son had bad blood.

Frank's wife was responsible, of course. Her Southern over-mothering had ruined the boy. She protected him from everyone, including Frank, she lied about his progress in school, she defended his crooked friends, covered up his scandals with girls, loaned him cars, gave him money and praised him endlessly.

It wasn't until she died, quite young, of cancer, that Frank found his main emotion was relief. David had never seemed to be his son at all. He belonged to his mother.

Then Frank met Rachael, a beautiful blue-eyed English woman, much younger than himself, honest and guileless, who ran a small advertising agency in Manhattan. She brought him new faith and joy, and he married her in less than a year.

David resented Rachael immediately.

His charm had no power over her. His temper was met by her equanimity. One night when his father was away and Rachael was alone, he tried a trick for which he was never forgiven.

Sodden with drink, he entered her bedroom. She fought him off easily.

His father didn't kick him out, but he was no longer welcome. Ignoring his son, Frank concentrated on his businesses, his new wife and his model-soldier war games played in his private study with fastidious historical accuracy.

12

Five years later, his father died, felled without warning by a sudden heart attack. Rachael was desolate.

The will was brief. Half a million dollars to the Injured Jockeys' Fund, his business fortune and stud interests to his beloved wife, Rachael.

David saw lawyers . . .

Mike poured White Horse into a tumbler and sniffed.

Easy does it, one day at a time.

He knew the first drink would have him back. It was the only drink he needed to stay away from. Hugo Latimer would love to see him fail.

Failure . . .

Sally had used that word, often. She saw how Hugo used him. When would he stand up for himself? She saw how his employer duped his owners, too.

James Brant paid high prices for horses worth nothing, which was easy enough in a world of backhanders and crooked dealing. Classic winners look like other horses. Who could tell?

Hugo talked well. He made owners believe him. He ran the best yard around and milked it to pay for his love of the tables in fashionable London casinos. Arabs handed him fortunes, until they began to suspect. Greeks used him for information. Former wives tried to make him pay. Bankers held charges on the Latimer Stables. Feed merchants waited for money. Staff turnover was high. Women were always on the telephone.

Hugo lived on the edge.

Mike left him after five years. He had worked hard at the yard, learning the trade. Once he became too tall and heavy to be a flat-race jockey, his first ambition, he decided to become the best trainer in racing.

Working his way up to Head Lad and then Assistant Trainer, Mike did everything he could to make the Latimer Stables succeed. Horses he picked and trained to win good races were used by Hugo to pull off betting 'jobs'. Hugo's needs were pressing. Owners were told that their best prospects were off form when they were beaten favourites.

The jobs were hidden from Mike. His transparent honesty was useful to Hugo. Mike did not know how to lie, and that made him valuable as a corroborator, or even a witness. Owners believed Mike more readily than they believed Hugo.

Hugo had been another reason for drinking . . .

Mike poured the whisky slowly back into the bottle.

He put it in a cupboard, moved papers roughly aside on his desk, and began working on the morning list.

It was a fine morning as Rachael Ware cantered over the skyline on her twenty-year-old hack and headed for home. The horse had been Frank's favourite gelding.

Frank had loved the Berkshire Downs. He became more English as he grew older. The Ware Stud, much smaller than his Kentucky farms, was the brightest jewel in his possession. The old house and stables, nestling close to Arkenfield in the valley below, the high expanses of springy turf above the chalk, where larks sing, tiny specks almost invisible in the wide sky above, was home to him.

Nearing the house, Rachael spotted John Grey's silver-blue Alvis turning in.

She liked John Grey and urged the old horse on.

He was a professional gambler who lived alone. Rachael fancied that she understood him. In his fifties, he was still handsome, with a full head of straight, fair hair and a dry sense of humour. Bachelor, scholar and eccentric, he had a fierce sense of independence, which she took to be defensive.

She was met by a young groom who took the reins as she dismounted.

'Cool him off, feed him, and turn him into the top paddock,' she ordered.

She turned, smiling, to where John Grey was getting out of the old car. Then she saw the passenger door open. Her face changed at once.

David Ware edged out.

'Rachael – ' he smiled, coldly.

'David . . . ? What on earth are you . . . ?'

She had not expected to see her stepson in England again.

David slung his bags over his shoulder and kissed her formally on the cheek.

'You know . . . I could murder a cup of tea.'

He walked to the front door, leaving Rachael angry and astonished. John Grey looked helpless.

'I took Mother to Heathrow. She's off again, to Atlantic City, or wherever. Came back to the car, and there he was. What could I do? Pretend I didn't know him?'

Rachael tossed her hair and turned towards the house.

'You might have run him over, John.'

High on the gallops, Mike stood with James Brant and Brigadier Forbes Collins, watching two horses canter over the rise towards them. The Brigadier, a racing stalwart, who lived life by the rule book, owned one of them, Vivid Dreams. He stared through military field glasses, clearly pleased that his was in the lead.

Lowering his glasses, he said to Brant, cheerfully, 'I'd say mine was helping yours along, old boy.'

Brant looked to Mike for support. Raw Silk was one of only two half-decent horses in his string. Mike's face gave nothing away.

'Both lads have been told to set 'em alight at the three-furlong marker.'

The horses approached the white marker-discs. The lads, Nick and Danny, urged them on and they galloped down past the group of watchers. Vivid Dreams increased his lead over Raw Silk. The Brigadier was delighted.

Brant's face was sour.

'Very, very nice,' said the Brigadier.

'Like to see him again?' Mike asked.

'No need. Keep him ticking over until Friday week.'

'James?'

Brant shook his head. As the two horses slowed and turned back towards them, he walked to the forty-year-old, mud-covered Land-Rover.

'I've seen enough.'

Mike knew he should have words of encouragement for Brant, because Raw Silk was a reasonable prospect, but he didn't know how to frame them. He turned instead to his two lads, who trotted up, waiting for more instructions.

'Once more and back to the yard. Let them jump off together, then quicken up on the bridle at the four pole.'

'Yes, Guv,' Nick shouted, cheerfully.

Mike followed his owners to the Land-Rover and climbed in behind the wheel. The Brigadier was beaming. Vivid Dreams had cost him eight thousand guineas, a bargain. Until he had been persuaded to bring the horse to Arkenfield, he thought it money lost.

'You've performed miracles, Mike,' he said, nudging Brant, 'what say you he gets a good price at Newbury?'

'A sure thing, I'd say,' Brant replied, sarcastically.

The old Land-Rover bumped and ground its way over the uneven turf towards the Arkenfield Yard, a mile away. Suddenly, it lurched and came to a standstill.

Mike cursed and switched off the engine. He flipped open the door and jumped out, walked round to the back and looked underneath, fearing the worst.

Brant and the Brigadier sat in silence.

The horses were cantering off in the distance towards the Ridgeway, which everyone knew as The Rudge. The wind blew against the sides of the old vehicle.

A minute later, Mike's face appeared in the doorway.

'Sorry, gents – you'll have to walk . . .'

Brant clenched his teeth and glared.

Rachael poured tea from a silver pot for David in the drawing room, where he sprawled, jet-lagged, with his feet up. John Grey watched her hand it across to him.

David was blithe, acting glad to be home again.

'Three years of hamburgers and squeaky-clean women is enough. So, here I am.'

'To stay?' Rachael dreaded his answer.

'Yes,' said David, decisively.

'Where?'

'The family pile, for the time being.'

Rachael looked at John Grey, mortified. He tried to be cool and practical, in her support.

'What about a job . . .?'

David sipped his tea.

'Pity to waste a Kentucky apprenticeship. I could make a contribution around here. Reorganize the breeding programme . . .'

Rachael rose to the bait, but contained herself.

'. . . but, you know, with my other commitments . . .

17

David rummaged in one of his bags and brought out a glossy promotional brochure. He tossed it casually on the table.

'. . . I won't have the time.'

Rachael hesitated, then picked it up.

The front cover read:

From ZDL
EQUAID
Turns Runners Into Winners

Two days later, Mike read the same brochure in his office. David scattered some small pellets from a sample bag on his desk. James Brant picked a few up and looked at them.

David's salesmanship was offhand and low-key, as if conferring a favour.

'Basically, it's a high-energy feed supplement.'

Mike was suspicious. He picked up a pellet, and sniffed it.

'What's in it?'

'Oh, the usual. Plus a secret herbal mix.'

Mike pushed the pellets away. He was not interested.

James Brant studied the opening paragraphs of the brochure, keeping an open mind, to Mike's annoyance.

David feigned unconcern.

'All above board. You don't get more respectable than ZDL – they've had it on sale in The States for months.'

He could see that Brant was absorbed in the slickly written copy which was slanted to American owners willing to try anything new.

His words were light.

'Results have been sensational.'

Mike, who knew David well, was not taken in any more.

'Why offer it just to me? Why not flood the market?'

'I'm a lazy bastard.'

David waited, letting Brant read more.

'I've got the UK franchise. If you put a couple of average horses on it and they start winning . . .'

'We do your advertising . . . Sorry, David, I don't think so.'

David gathered the pellets back into the sample bag and shrugged. He didn't seem to care.

'Hold on a minute. What if we put one horse on it?'

James Brant was sold.

David smiled kindly at Mike, for Brant's benefit, and said with charm 'I'm not suggesting an alternative to your training regime, Mike. Look upon Equaid as a way of maximizing potential. Putting one over on the opposition . . .'

He knew his customer. James Brant was suddenly eager.

'Let's face it – Raw Silk needs all the help she can get,' he said to Mike, who turned his head away in disgust.

David tossed in his clincher.

'Give it a month. If you're not satisfied, I'll give you your money back. Can I say fairer?'

Frances Ross was the daughter of a top National Hunt jockey whose bones had been crushed in a fall towards the end of the previous season. Her mother died when she was a baby. She had no knowledge of her, except a few photographs and what her father said.

Jack Ross had been her father and mother. He was the most important person in her life.

She told herself that when she went to live in America it was for sound career reasons. She had a biochemistry degree and wanted to advance breeding and bloodstock in

19

the best laboratories in the world, refusing to allow herself to think that she needed to escape from her father to live a life of her own.

During her three years on the big blue-grass ranches, Frances was happy and free and able to make her own mistakes. She was still in her twenties, bright and very attractive, with forthright views and ideas of her own. She loved Americans and their positive attitudes.

She loved one American in particular.

She wrote every week to her father, telling him how fine everything was, even when her affair went badly wrong. She telephoned as often as she could, surprised at how near he sounded. She was proud of him winning races into his fifties, after breaking almost every bone in his body during his long career.

She wished he would meet someone. He was still powerful, with light-brown hair and a weather-lined face, trim and athletic, and she hated the thought of him living alone.

Then Jack Ross fell in a steeplechase and landed badly. The horse twisted and crashed on top of him. St John Ambulance were there in seconds, the vet following in his car close behind. Jack was carefully eased on to a stretcher and driven very slowly to hospital, while the vet felt the horse's pastern bones. They were shattered, like a bag of marbles. Canvas screens were hurriedly pulled round the screaming animal to conceal it from the race crowds. The vet pulled his revolver from his raincoat pocket and shot the horse in the brain.

Beside Frances' bed in Kentucky before dawn, the telephone rang. She was back in England later the same day.

Jack Ross was in a wheelchair when he signed himself out of hospital, but he was determined to do away with it as soon as he got home. He ignored the advice of doctors and walked painfully, a few steps a day, suffering despair and waves of depression. But he was an expert in broken bones, and was not frightened of them.

His sole aim was to get back up on a horse.

Frances knew better than to forbid him openly. She had the same stubborn streak, and she saw that hope brightened her father's mood and humoured him. She was equally determined that he would never go near a horse again.

Jack Ross was out on the roads, dressed in a track-suit, timing his slow progress with a stop-watch, when the Ware Stud's green Range Rover, driven fast on the wrong side of the lane, forced him to jump aside. He cursed the driver before recognizing who it was.

It didn't stop, which was no more than he expected.

He told Frances as soon as he got home to the tiny cottage and saw her face harden. David Ware's name was unpopular everywhere.

'Why did he single you out?' Frances asked Mike, while they were both leaning on the paddock gate that afternoon, watching Raw Silk cropping grass.

'We go back a bit. He was always around,' said Mike, who seemed evasive to her.

'After you split up with your wife?'

Mike didn't reply and she apologized for the intrusion. They knew each other too well and were both careful.

'I was drinking then. David's a great one for exploiting anyone's weakness. He must've thought I'd be easier to persuade than most.'

'Which you were,' said Frances, looking at the horse.

'Brant swallowed the patter, not me. I wanted to show

21

him the door. But, if it keeps him off my back for a week or two . . .'

Raw Silk edged closer to them, munching peacefully. She was in fine condition.

A week later, there was an improvement. Raw Silk's speed on the gallops was up by four seconds, over a measured distance. She seemed to take more interest in her work. Joe Hogan, Mike's Head Lad, reported her eating up well and Nick, who rode her in training, pronounced her a different horse.

'Full of herself,' said Nick, who had plans to be a trainer himself one day. 'Worked like she wants a trip.'

Mike did not believe in too many additives. He had firm ideas about spring water, fresh bruised Scottish oats or barley, carrots, turnips, and carefully chosen cubes of vitamins and minerals. His horses were fed little and often and were checked constantly.

But he rang Brant to report that Equaid seemed to be having a good effect, because he was glad to give good news, to make up for the usual excuses. Brant quickly raised hopes of winning a race at Kempton.

Rachael Ware was wary when Mike called, asking to see David.

'What's he done?'

'Nothing. I wanted to tell him that Equaid appears to be just as good as he said.'

She was relieved, but not convinced. David still thought that the farms in Kentucky and the Ware Stud should belong to him.

'He believes I persuaded Frank to cut him out of his

22

will. I didn't,' she said, when Mike wondered if David had changed.

David Ware had not changed. They both knew that.

But what was he up to?

Stewart Staunton, the vet, was called urgently to Arkenfield next morning to treat Raw Silk for injury. The horse had spooked at a door banging in the wind, by the covered manège and Nick had been thrown off. Mike caught the reins after the horse had whipped round and collided heavily with the wall. It kicked in pain, but Mike held on.

Nick was unhurt.

'What happened?' asked Brant, more interested in his horse.

'Don't know, sir,' said Nick. 'She's been jumpy for a day or two. Smallest thing sets her off.'

Then they saw the filly's foreleg. It had spread a plate and was holding its injured foot off the ground.

Staunton said there was no serious damage. All that was needed was a poultice boot for the bruising and time to heal and Raw Silk would be fine.

'What about Kempton?'

The vet would not commit himself.

Brant followed Staunton to his car and smiled, pleasantly.

'I know there's nothing you can do to speed the healing process,' he said, taking out his wallet.

'That's right.'

'But what about something for the pain?'

The vet looked at him suspiciously.

'I'm not sure I understand you . . .'

The smile was unchanged.

23

'Oh, come on, Stewart. Something to take her mind off it. You know what I mean. So she can run.'

A shadow moved across the open doorway of the feed-house nearby.

Joe Hogan strained to hear Staunton's reply.

After evening stables that night, Mike went to the Dog. As usual he wanted a beer or a whisky, but he drank orange juice and hated it.

John Grey stood in his corner and sympathized.

There was nothing to be done. Horses were always having illnesses or accidents.

'How did Brant take it?'

'Surprisingly well,' said Mike, suddenly finding Brant's reaction odd.

He was wondering about this, when more early-doors customers came in. Jack Ross walked carefully up to the bar and ordered a round. Frances was with him and that meant retelling the story. Other stories followed, as they always did in the Dog, and Mike began to feel better, as he listened.

He decided that giving up alcohol was no reason to stay out of the pub, where he had always been part of the racing crowd.

Stewart Staunton examined Raw Silk's leg again the next day and said it was fit to run. When Brant heard the news in his office, he was delighted and started making arrangements for Kempton. He called Kath first, and was dismayed to hear that she had other plans. His wife did not share his obsession with racing. He wanted her to stand with him in the Winner's Enclosure, but this was only a small race and he could wait.

*

But he missed her being with him on the great day when he had his first winner. He jumped for joy when Raw Silk romped home with a clear lead over six other horses. His horse had won!

'And at six to one, as well!' he roared, reaching for the champagne and heading, with Mike, for the prize-giving ceremony in front of the Weighing Room. Desultory claps applauded his victory.

There were few onlookers. The tiny vase was only a token, the prize money was small change to him. The television cameras were at another meeting. The commentator was already giving the runners and riders in the next, but Brant knew the glorious feeling of being a winning owner. He was even more excited than he had been in his shrewd deals in the early days of building his empire, when his blood was up.

John Grey congratulated them after the weigh-in.

'At the price, David Ware had a good touch . . .' he commented to Mike, thoughtfully. 'Ten thousand at sixes . . .'

Something was wrong.

Celebrations at Arkenfield were joyous. Nick was tipped on the muck-heap, a great honour.

Mike spoke to David about further supplies of Equaid and wondered if it would benefit all the rags in his charge.

David made odd, weak excuses.

Customs and Excise were checking his consignments. There were blue forms and green forms.

They were checking for dope.

Until he had clearance, all the Equaid in England was impounded at the dock-side.

He was only a salesman, with his samples.

*

Networks of friends in racing work the favour system. Mike heard from his friend Steve Matthews, who now worked for Weatherby's. Steve's wife had left him, despite aerobics and counselling and sharing the housework. He and Mike played squash together.

'No details. Your horse, Raw Silk – '

'Yes?'

' – it's failed the routine drug test . . .'

'What?'

'Gotta go.'

Mike checked with his Head Lad, Joe Hogan.

'You kept samples?'

'From every batch, one from each feed, for the regulation six weeks, as you said.'

'Must be the Equaid.'

Joe seemed to have other ideas.

Stewart Staunton was angry, as he listened to Mike's accusation.

'Who told you that?'

'Doesn't matter.'

'It does to me.'

'Are you denying that Brant asked you to treat a horse with a banned substance? What was it? Bute?'

Staunton brushed his receding hair with his hand.

'He offered me a thousand pounds to get Raw Silk ready for Kempton. I told him the same as I've told countless other owners and trainers . . .'

He walked to the door, showing Mike out of his surgery.

'Shouldn't you have said something to me?'

Staunton paused, his hand on the doorknob.

'Yes, probably . . .'

'Then why the hell didn't you?'

There was an awkward pause. Stewart Staunton was a young vet in a small partnership, seeking to specialize in horses.

'If you really want to know, I thought you may have put him up to it . . .' he ventured.

The substance was Stanazolol, a steroid. Mike was ordered to appear before the Disciplinary Committee of the Jockey Club, who had the power to ban him for life. The racing press ran a story.

Brigadier Forbes Collins read the *Sporting Life* and the *Racing Post*. He withdrew Vivid Dreams from Arkenfield at once, fearing the whiff of scandal.

But surprisingly the samples of Equaid tested were cleared.

'Standard feed mix. Vitamin and mineral supplements similar to other proprietary brands,' the laboratory report said.

The drug could not be traced to a source in the Arkenfield yard.

That night Mike questioned his staff once more.

A trainer is held to be responsible for his horses. Even without evidence, he could still lose his licence.

Joe Hogan was Mike's Head Lad, and had worked with him at Latimer's for years. Joe was honest, a good judge of horses, but lacking courage on his own behalf. He once had ideas of becoming a trainer himself, but his nerve failed. He preferred to work in the background and let others push their names forward.

He wanted to leave Latimer's when Mike left, but held on, avoiding the decision, until Hugo sacked him for moonlighting, because he helped Mike too much in his spare time.

Mike watched, with Frances and John Grey, as Joe laid out the samples of Equaid on the bench in the feed-house. Each was labelled, in a plastic envelope. John Grey was impressed.

'Do you always keep a sample from every bag?'

'No. Each batch, usually. Mike told me to make an exception with this.'

'The investigators sampled every one?'

Joe nodded.

'First batch and second batch.'

Frances looked at Mike, questioning.

'Second batch?'

'David replenished our stock,' Mike explained.

'Before the race, or after?'

'After,' said Joe, 'I gave him a hand unloading.'

'So you were with him the whole time?'

'No,' he said, suddenly, remembering that the farrier had called during David's visit. 'I was out in the yard a minute, looking at a split hoof . . .'

'Leaving David Ware alone . . . Here, with these samples?'

'For a minute or two . . .'

Mike's eyes gleamed.

'First batch – what happened to the empty bags?'

'On the dump,' Joe replied, carefully, 'same as always . . .'

Frances drove Mike over to Stewart Staunton's with the empty bags they had rescued from the dump. He was going to apologize and sought in his mind for the right words.

28

'Shall I come in with you?' asked Frances, as she stopped her Rover in the courtyard, the sign reflecting the headlights.

S. Staunton & Partners
Veterinary Surgeons

Mike shook his head. It was going to be hard enough, without her listening. He lifted a few of the Equaid sacks off the back seat, spilling grains.

'Careful!' said Frances, 'There's hardly enough to test as it is.'

Mike got out and paused.

'Frances?'

'Yes?'

'All the trouble you've taken . . . I appreciate it.'

She watched him walk to the lighted front door. Stewart Staunton lived over the surgery.

Mike rang the bell and waited.

Frances saw Staunton's face as he opened the door, looking grim. The two men talked on the step for five minutes. She watched anxiously. Then they shook hands and went inside, still talking.

She sat back in her seat and waited.

A full moon hung over Arkenfield. Security lamps shone dimly in the yard. Joe Hogan was visiting each box, mellow with beer, wondering about his future.

If Mike lost his licence at the Jockey Club hearing next morning, he would be out of a job.

He had no money and no home. His wife, too, had left him, years ago, sick of his drinking and gambling. He had no children he knew of. His life had been spent in and around stables.

He supposed someone would give him a job, but not as Head Lad.

Hugo Latimer wouldn't give him a reference. Bad-mouth him instead, probably, if he was lucky enough to get an offer. But leaving a stable involved in a drugs scandal . . .

A car turned in, with dipped headlights. It was Mike and Frances returning. Joe worried about Mike more than himself. If he lost his trainer's licence there was no way back.

Mike got out. Joe heard him say something to Frances, but he couldn't catch what. He wondered if they might make a pair.

The Rover purred away, leaving Mike standing in the yard.

Joe walked slowly over to him, whistling tunelessly.

After midnight, Frances talked on the telephone, in her tiny office, which was once a bedroom. She kept her voice low because she thought her father was asleep next door.

Jack heard her voice.

'No problems with Equaid anywhere in the States?'

He got up stiffly and wrapped himself in his dressing-gown as he listened to half a conversation. He knew Frances was ringing her friends in Kentucky.

'What? David? When was that? Do you think Bill Bourdon would talk to me? What's his number? Thanks, Ray . . .'

Jack opened his bedroom door.

It was early in the morning in Kentucky.

He thought he would go downstairs and make coffee, expecting to be up all night.

Bright sun shone through the window at Arkenfield as

Mike peered at himself in a cracked mirror. He wore his only suit, which Sally had chosen, and a white shirt. He retied his tie and brushed off his shoulders. He wished he had slept.

A car horn sounded, approaching the yard, and he peered out of a small dirty window to see John Grey's old open-topped Alvis drawing up below.

A quick look at the photograph of his son, Tom, then he picked up his scuffed briefcase from the bed and hurried downstairs.

John Grey leaned across and opened the passenger door.

'Has Staunton called?' he asked, with eager concern.

'No.'

Mike tossed the briefcase behind the seats and climbed in.

'Clutching at straws, John. Let's get on with it.'

The immaculately kept old car slid forward out of the lane, through the village and towards the motorway.

42, Portman Square, London, the headquarters of the Jockey Club, is a featureless modern building on the south side. Mike and John Grey parked in a garage and walked over the square to the glass doors and went up in the lift to the second floor.

The trim receptionist asked them to wait and picked up the telephone. She was cheerful and efficient, which added to their fears.

Behind her, the bronze of Tagalie, the only filly to win both the One Thousand Guineas and the Derby, stood proudly looking at them.

They sat in silence on low sofas beneath gilt-framed oils of long-ago racehorses. Jockey Club staff passed by, unconcernedly going about their business. The lift doors opened and closed, with periodic visitors.

A tall man in a dark blue pin-stripe suit came over and introduced himself as the Secretary to the Disciplinary Committee. He asked Mike to follow him.

John Grey watched as Mike trailed after the tall man down the corridor towards a door which had the lighted sign: COMMITTEE ROOM — MEETING IN PROGRESS.

He stood up, rubbed his chin, and took keen interest in a huge painting of a steeplechaser flying over a towering fence.

Frances was asleep, with her head on her desk. Jack sat uncomfortably in a chair, raising and lowering his leg. They had stayed awake all night, waiting for the telephone to ring, but it was now too late to help Mike.

It was ten in the morning. The hearing had begun.

Suddenly, the telephone rang.

The room was small and oblong, with plain walls, racing pictures and a screened-off area which concealed video-tapes of races. The windows did not look out over the square, but faced other plain, anonymous offices at the back.

The Committee sat behind two sides of a dog-leg desk covered in blue baize, the Chairman and two Members on one leg, the secretary, Investigating Officer, Jockey Club lawyer and an analyst on the other. Recording microphones stood before them.

Mike sat facing them, alone. He had decided not to employ a lawyer.

The Chairman said, pleasantly, 'You understand, Mr Hardy, that these proceedings are an enquiry, not a trial?'

Mike smiled wryly.

'Yes, Mr Chairman. I'm in breach of Rules 53 and 180. I'm not denying that.'

One of the Members was a middle-aged woman, with a sharp face.

'Difficult, under the circumstances,' she said, cuttingly.

The Chairman looked at her.

'Mrs Maxwell?'

'A steroid was found in all three samples, randomly taken and numbered. The laboratories can't tell which sample is taken from which horse. Our procedures are scientific and completely fair. This is a steroid used by human athletes. A very serious matter, Mr Chairman.'

Mike sensed that he already had an enemy on the Committee.

He glanced to one side, towards a young man with thinning hair.

'Yes, but your investigating officer hasn't said how it got there.'

'We await your explanation, Mr Hardy.'

'I haven't got one.'

The Committee Members waited a moment, exchanging looks. They were not pleased with Mike's blunt honesty. They were used to hearing skilled advocates with polished arguments.

'Would you care to expand?' the Chairman asked, his pleasantness fading.

'I can't,' said Mike, simply.

The three Members looked at him closely, not liking this.

'Flippancy won't help your case, Mr Hardy,' the Chairman said.

'I'm not being flippant!' Mike snapped, without thinking. He struggled to control himself, searching for words.

'My livelihood is at stake here,' he said, more quietly. 'I want to keep my licence. But all I can say is this. No one at Arkenfield was involved in doping Raw Silk.'

The Members looked at the Investigating Officer.

He looked at his notes.

The analyst sniffed, scratched his ear and played with a pencil.

The Chairman began to look pleasant again. A moment later, he leaned forward and smiled.

'Your honesty does you credit . . .' he said.

'It does indeed,' Mrs Maxwell added.

Mike felt a momentary surge of hope.

Then the Chairman leant back. He spoke in a controlled voice, his smile vanishing.

'. . . but it hardly constitutes an adequate defence . . .'

John Grey had been called to the telephone at the reception desk. He was hastily scribbling notes on a scrap of paper.

'What? You're sure? Will Tom Bourdon put that in writing . . .?'

The lift doors opened and Stewart Staunton stepped out, eyes alight, looking flustered and breathing heavily.

'Bloody traffic, bloody parking . . . Sorry to cut it so fine.'

John Grey put the telephone down, pleased.

'Stewart – that was Frances. We've got something, at least. What about you?'

'Just get me in there,' said Stewart, urgently.

The Committee listened.

'Samples of the first batch bags were contaminated. Here

34

is the Public Analyst's report.' Staunton handed a paper over the desk.

The Members looked at it in turn.

'You mean the samples kept by the Head Lad were exchanged?' the Chairman enquired.

The vet nodded.

'Before they were taken by your investigator, yes.'

The Investigating Officer reached over for the report and shared reading it with the analyst.

John Grey stood up.

'Gentlemen, Mrs Maxwell,' he said, 'in support of that evidence, it has come to light that the person who supplied the Equaid feed supplement to Mr Hardy was recently involved in an identical incident in the United States.'

Mrs Maxwell knew John Grey.

'They have a different attitude to drugs. Was it reported?'

'It was discovered before the horse ran.'

'Can it be confirmed?'

'Tom Bourdon will fax a statement to the Jockey Club today.'

The American name was well known in international racing. Mrs Maxwell was determined to demonstrate her impartiality.

'May we have the name of the person?'

John Grey looked at Mike, who immediately said, 'David Ware.'

Eyebrows were raised slightly.

'Frank Ware's son?'

'Yes.'

The Committee were silent. Frank Ware's memory was hallowed and they were distressed by this accusation. It would need careful corroboration. They also knew his widow.

'We will adjourn for lunch,' said the Chairman, rising.

Frances drove up to the Ware Stud. She was tired, but too angry to rest until she had confronted David Ware.

He listened to her accusations in front of Rachael, padding round the panelled drawing room, showing little concern.

'Oh, Tom Bourdon,' he said, dismissively. 'He has a personal grudge. He'd say anything.'

Frances had other names.

'Ray Trotter? Pete Hampson? Sidney Bach?'

David remained unimpressed.

'Kentucky Mafia,' he scoffed. 'We all know they stick together.'

Frances looked to Rachael for support, but she said nothing.

'You both know Mike could lose his licence,' said Frances, coldly.

David Ware shrugged, as if helpless.

'I supplied him with a feed supplement made by one of the best-known companies in the world. It's great. What's wrong with that?'

Frances saw an opportunity.

'So when he sues ZDL, for selling him a contaminated product, you won't mind when their investigators knock on your door?'

David sat down.

'Why me? Mike Hardy has more to gain.'

'And lose.'

'You've got something going, have you?'

'What?'

36

'You and Mike?'

Rachael could see Frances stiffen with anger.

'That's enough David,' she said. 'In my house—'

'My father's house!' David Ware flared.

'No. Mine.' Her tone was level.

Frank Ware's equestrian portrait stared down from above the fireplace.

The meeting of the Disciplinary Committee reconvened after lunch. What had been discussed in the interim Mike did not know. The fax had arrived in the meantime, confirming Tom Bourdon's statement in detail.

The Chairman acknowledged this in his preamble and went on to say, 'Our unanimous decision,' he paused to take in Mrs Maxwell, 'is to disqualify Raw Silk from first place at Kempton . . . and to delay any action against you, until the tests carried out by the Public Analyst can be confirmed by our own laboratory . . . until then, you may continue training at Arkenfield.'

Mike sat, impassively.

Inside, he was shrieking with joy.

Racing journalists wanted statements as soon as they got out. Mike made no comment and hurried past them, out on to Portman Square, followed by John Grey and Stewart Staunton. It was not an acquittal. It had not been a trial. Their best assessment was that it would result in a fine, or a severe warning about security in the yard, or both.

'I've still lost an owner,' said Mike, managing to sound ungrateful, he thought afterwards.

When they got back to the yard, the staff were celebrating.

A new silver Land-Rover Discovery stood by his office. Lettering on the side matched the board.

ARKENFIELD STABLES
Trainer Michael Hardy

'Arrived after you called from the Jockey Club,' Joe grinned. 'With the compliments of Mr Brant.'

James Brant came out of the office, with champagne and glasses and set them on the snub nose of the new vehicle. He poured a glass for Mike.

'Is this contrition?' whispered John Grey, a little too loudly.

'Contrition?' Brant laughed. 'Investment. I'm not built for walking back from the gallops.'

Mike spoke to Rachael, later, on the telephone. His voice was hard.

'Equaid . . . the rest of it, where does he keep it?'

It was growing dark. Mike's new Discovery, spattered with mud, was parked near a barn on the Ware estate. A few sacks of Equaid were stacked outside, ten yards from the building.

Mike dragged the last of the sacks out into the open. Then he spotted a small plastic-wrapped package.

He picked it up, opened it and sniffed the contents.

Over the rise, he heard a vehicle approaching. The green Range Rover of the Ware Stud roared towards him on the dirt road, raising a plume.

Mike ran to the back of the Discovery and opened the door. He took out a red polythene petrol container. He unscrewed the cap, sprinkled petrol over the sacks, and struck a match. A sudden blaze flowered.

38

David Ware in the Range Rover skidded to a halt as the flames rose higher.

'What the hell do you think you're doing?' he shouted, furiously.

'Making sure,' said Mike, watching the growing inferno.

'I've sold that stuff!'

Mike held the package out.

'I'm turning this over to the Jockey Club, David.'

David Ware moved quickly. He grabbed the package from Mike's hand and threw it into the heart of the blaze.

The evidence had gone.

Mike swung his fist at David. He missed, then struck again in fury, as David backed away, mocking him.

Mike caught him on the jaw, knocking him backwards into the fire.

David cried out, as the flames took hold of his clothes. Mike stood back and watched as he coughed and beat himself in panic. Then he rolled clear and lay in the dust, dousing the smoking scorch-marks and wiping blood from his lip.

Mike stood over him.

Then he turned and walked slowly back to his new vehicle.

TWO

Charles Burton, MP, owned Dangerous Lady, a brown filly by Green For Danger out of Ladysmith. She was an improving two-year-old.

Mike liked her immediately.

Bought as a yearling at Goff's by an owner who sold her on, she was shipped over from Ireland, with a reputation for bad temper. Frances had spotted her as a fourteen-thousand-guinea bargain for one of her clients. Mike suspected that the horse had been ill-treated.

Her new owner hardly ever visited the yard. He didn't telephone constantly to check on her progress. His cheques were regular and he raised no queries about extra charges for veterinary or farrier's fees.

Instead, Mike was left alone to get on with job of training a very nervous animal who showed sprinting ability. But she was unpredictable and the lads were wary of her. She spooked on the gallops and kicked in the box and they all thought she was well named.

When Mike entered her in a five-furlong dash, he informed the owner, who was not in. He left a message with his wife.

His call was not returned, so he was surprised when the fifty-year-old Member of Parliament turned up at the course.

His wife, Anna, was with him, holding his arm.

Her wide-brimmed straw hat, with its brown ribbon, concealed her face until she tilted her head back. She looked about forty, but Mike knew she was older. She was pretty and slim, with warm laughing brown eyes; strong face, thought Mike, who admired her.

Charles Burton had aged. A few months ago, his name had been news. A financial scandal had cut off his chance of a front-bench seat. Allegations of insider dealing, never proven, led to a press hunt, which lasted for weeks. He was too good-looking to be blameless, they thought, but they found no evidence of sexual iniquity. So they made the most of his love of racing and drinking.

But he and Anna were both cheerful, enjoying every moment of their day at the races. Burton looked thinner, Mike thought. He had an indoor, late-night, overworked colour. Was there some truth in the drinking stories? Was he damaging his health, as they said?

Their pleasure was shared and they acted like lovers. Mike felt a pang of envy as he took them over to the centre of the parade ring. The runners, slender two-year-olds, not yet fully formed, circled the green lawn, led by their lads, as the crowds outside pressed and peered. The bright early May sun lit the colourful new dresses and hats. Brown trilbies were relieved by a few panamas and the air was filled with the excitement of spring and the new flat season.

'Don't get your hopes up,' said Mike, 'I'll be happy if she's in the first six.'

There were only five runners.

Security men stood at the gates dividing the stands, keeping the Members' Enclosure free from Tattersalls, where the bookies had their joints set up in rows. Beyond more gates, the mass in the Silver Ring stretched far away from the winning post.

One of them spotted a girl of nineteen or twenty, dressed in jeans and blue T-shirt, swing over the high coping of the perimeter wall. She dropped and disappeared into the crowd.

Mo Ratcliffe, a sparky, blue-eyed, five-foot-four fireball, grabbed hold of the white plastic rail and cheered wildly as the horses cantered out to the start.

'Come on, Lady!' she shouted, waving her arms.

Dangerous Lady tossed her head. Mo was quite sure the horse had heard her.

At the start, the five runners circled as their girths were checked. Dangerous Lady had to be hooded to be led into her stall, and was last in, but she got out well when the gates sprang open.

The favourite ran to the front and stayed there. Dangerous Lady was third, looking for room on the rail, well in contention, leaving a clear gap ahead of the other two. In the last furlong, the course commentator quickened his voice excitedly and the crowds yelled as she drove to take second place, a length behind.

Mo Ratcliffe dodged past flocking people as the announcements were made and headed for the Winner's Enclosure, punching the air with delight.

Dangerous Lady did not seem to want to stand in the stall marked Second in front of the Weighing Room. She reared and frightened the onlookers.

Mo's voice called out, 'I knew you could do it, Lady! You will do it!'

In the packed Owners' and Trainers' Bar five minutes later, Charles Burton walked over to a table, with a magnum of champagne. Mike and Frances cleared a space and rearranged the chairs. John Grey, who had backed the third horse to win, joined them, putting on a brave face.

'If this is for second, what do we get when she wins?' Frances shouted above the noise.

Anna Burton filled one of the glasses with orange juice. For a second, Mike was embarrassed, but she handed it to her husband. He topped it with champagne.

When he had poured the others a glass each, he raised his own.

'To the Lady!' he called out.

They toasted the horse. Mike took a sip.

'And to you, Mike! When's the next?'

'Frances, not me. She spotted her.'

'Miss Ross, I'm forever grateful,' said Burton, kissing her hand with great charm and making her blush.

He sounded sincere.

Mike moved closer to him.

'There's a race coming up we might go for . . .'

Mo Ratcliffe followed the Arkenfield team back to the stables on her motor bike, keeping well behind.

She did not know the Berkshire Downs. She had not seen much of the English countryside. Her childhood had been spent moving from Hulme to Wythenshawe and back, with her depressed mother. For months, Mo was 'in care', living in hostels. Then she stayed with a succession of foster parents in other parts of Greater Manchester. A small daughter of one of them loved horses and never stopped talking about them.

Staff at the inner-city Job Centre were intrigued when

Mo asked about a career with horses. They persuaded the British Racing School to give her one of the 150 places on their stablecraft course.

She spent nine weeks at Newmarket, working every day, learning the basics of riding, grooming and mucking-out the thirty-odd thoroughbreds kept at the school. She loved every minute and passed all the tests well.

She was placed with trainers for a while in yards around Newmarket and then signed with Michael O'Shea as apprentice jockey, in Ireland.

At the beginning of her second year there, she met Dangerous Lady. The horse was as backward and troublesome as she had been, and still was. They took to each other at once.

Mo clenched the clutch and handbrake and changed down with her foot as she saw the horsebox swing into a tight lane, lined with hedges. Skidding to a halt, she watched it manoeuvre slowly into the yard. She had found The Lady's new home.

She revved and killed the engine, took off her helmet and sat back, legs astride, working out what to do next.

The filly kicked and reared as soon as she came down the ramp. The commotion set the other horses off and alarmed a syndicate of owners present, who each had a share in one horse. They kept well back, as Dangerous Lady was boxed and listened to the continuous cries of distress as she hammered the walls inside, venting spite and screaming.

'Right little cow, sometimes, she can be,' said Mo, 'But I can handle her.'

'Who are you?' asked Mike, turning to the strange girl who had appeared behind him.

'Maureen Ratcliffe, sir,' said Mo. 'I was apprenticed to Mick O'Shea and I looked after The Lady. I know her. Open up and I'll show you. She'll hurt herself if you don't!'

Mike hesitated, then glanced at Joe. He had one eye on the syndicate, who looked worried.

'Do as she says.'

Joe went to the box, cautiously. He opened the half-door just enough to let Mo slide through and bolted it again quickly, top and bottom.

'Hallo, Lady,' said Mo.

Mike and Joe listened as she chattered, softly. The kicking and screaming stopped. There was silence.

A few moments later, Mo called for Joe to free the bolts, opened the door and led the horse out into the yard, where she walked round snorting peacefully, shoving at Mo with her nose.

'No secret,' said Mo. 'Bit of kindness, that's all.'

She was given a three-month trial. Mike rang the Kildare trainer to check, but he was away. Mike questioned her carefully and watched her ride, noticing her affinity with Dangerous Lady. She was his best horse. He started to wonder if she was the good horse he was searching for, the first one.

Charles Burton surprised him by turning up at the gallops before eight one morning the following week, by himself. The sky was clear, the blackthorn snowed with blossom. Larks hung high above and meadow pipits rose from the ground. Breathing the air in deeply, Burton slapped his arms against his sides and watched them ride work, smiling, lost in a world of his own. Dangerous Lady was catching pigeons, with Mo on her back, riding superbly, in front of Black Deed.

'If you knew how much this means to me . . .' he said, quietly.

Mo lived with the lads in the Hilton, the scruffy quarters over the stables. She was given The Lady, as one of her two. Danny resented her because of this. He had ideas of becoming Arkenfield's apprentice jockey and was constantly pressing his claim. He goaded her and she spat back fearlessly, ready to take him on, despite finding out that he was a useful amateur boxer.

She had her own room, with a lock on the door. She had her own grooming kit, which she let no one touch. She ignored the taunts and sexual banter, or gave back as good as she got, and devoted herself to the job.

Black Deed, by Black Spot out of Noble Nancy, was also well named. A big, honest bay, owned by James Brant, one of two in his string worth the feed. Mike had trained him at Latimer's since the day the colt arrived from the Sales.

Hugo Latimer had built him up as a Classic prospect to James Brant, who paid accordingly. Mike saw him as a winner of a few minor races, but went along with the game by keeping his mouth shut. As Hugo's assistant, he often had to say nothing. All his eight horses were earmarked for Group races, but needed more time. Meanwhile, Brant paid the high fees, watched them eat and believed the excuses.

Black Deed ran at Newbury, the previous season. With nothing to beat him, he started favourite.

Brant's wife Kath joined him, for once, to share his great day.

Hugo sent Mike to a meeting in Chester, over a hundred miles away. Then he changed the jockey to an apprentice and gave new instructions on how to ride the race. It was easy enough. The horse went to the front too early. There was no evidence on the closed-circuit screen of it being pulled up. Black Deed ran the wrong race as hard as he could and he did well to be second.

Bookmakers paid out a lot of money, to Hugo's indirect benefit.

Brant was furious.

Hugo soothed him by blaming Mike. That was easy, too. The drinking was obvious. A few words of sympathy about Mike's domestic problems, garnished with praise for his natural ability, and Brant would simmer down, because there were always other races for his talented string. What did Brant know about horses?

Hugo miscalculated. Mike left in disgust when he found out. He wanted to report Hugo to the Stewards of the Jockey Club, but would they believe him? Hugo was a well-established trainer. What was he? A bitter young man with a grievance, out of a job.

Others were suspicious of Hugo. Words were said on telephones and in corners. Joe Hogan spoke to John Grey. John Grey spoke to Rachael Ware. Rachael Ware spoke to Kath Brant . . .

James Brant took all his horses away from the Latimer yard.

That was the start of Arkenfield.

Rachael Ware had a small financial stake in the new venture. She also paid the wages of a secretary, Rosie Carson, a sharp-eyed woman in her thirties, known as 'The Dragon' in the village, because of her fearsome, fiery tongue. Married to Stan Carson, she needed it to defend herself. She performed office duties: wages, insurances, vaccinations, entries and declarations, accounts, and made excuses to owners. Mike thought her main function was to keep an eye on him.

'Mr James Brant phoned,' said Rosie, 'checking you're not neglecting Black Deed. He's coming to watch work in the morning.'

Black Deed and Dangerous Lady were cantering upsides on the wide green sea of the Downs beneath the big sky. Mo held The Lady back and shouted to Nick who was on Black Deed, 'Go on, then. Give the Guv'nor something to smile about.'

Nick grinned. He urged Black Deed into a gallop ahead of the Lady and widened the gap as they passed Mike and Brant.

'That was worth getting up for.' Brant was well pleased.

'Glad you liked it.'

'Make sure there are no mishaps before Saturday. You know Hugo's entered Morgana's Bane?'

'Yes.'

'Good horse.'

'I know.'

'See you Saturday,' said Brant, happily.

He walked off towards his white BMW, as the two horses returned, steaming.

'Great performance,' said Mike, drily. 'You should be on the stage, both of you.'

They laughed.

'Go on, get Second Lot sorted.'

Mike opened the door of his Land-Rover, a determined look on his face.

James Brant went through a list of names. Clients, friends, those he needed to impress. He spent an hour ringing them.

'Yes, Bath. I've taken a box. Laid on a spot of lunch. Should be a good day out.'

He smiled, modestly.

'Black Deed in the first. All I can say is he's done everything asked of him in training . . .'

Kath heard him making the calls and warned him.

'But Mike says he's a cert – well, not in so many words . . .'

'You could lose a lot of friends, James.'

At midnight on Friday, Mike sat alone in the office, working, when he heard a noise in the yard outside. Peering through the window, he saw a shadow move across the front of the boxes.

He opened the door and slipped quietly out, but saw nobody. He stood listening.

Then he heard a shuffling sound. The shape of a man approached The Lady's box.

Alarmed, he ran across the made a grab. The figure cried out and turned. It was Joe Hogan, returning late from the Dog with a bottle.

''Strewth, Guv'nor . . .'

'Joe? What are you up to?'

'Thought I'd look in on The Lady . . .'

'You needn't bother.'

'Oh?'

Mike slipped open the bolts on The Lady's box, carefully. He pointed inside. Joe looked in.

Mo Ratcliffe lay curled in a blanket next to Dangerous Lady, fast asleep in the hay.

Mike closed the doors of the box again, as Joe shook his head, smiling. He took a swig from the bottle and set off towards the Hilton, muttering.

Mike walked slowly back to his office, under a full moon. A fox spoke in the Arkenfield paddock beyond.

M. Hardy, Arkenfield, appeared twice on the official race card. Mike had hopes for both his runners at Bath.

Black Deed led the opening sprint. James Brant's guests yelled, while his wife stayed calm. She stood next to Mike in the private box, watching reactions, eating a dry biscuit.

A challenger appeared. Morgana's Bane made ground, Black Deed fought back, the commentator raised his pitch. At the line, the crowds roared as Morgana's Bane won by a short head.

James Brant angrily turned to Mike.

'What the hell happened?'

'He came second . . .' said Mike, shortly.

He slipped out of the private box, heading for the unsaddling enclosure, leaving Brant fuming.

Kath smiled faintly, as her husband poured Mumm's to pacify his disappointed guests. They pretended not to mind.

Dangerous Lady won the four o'clock race.

But there were doubts, at first. She was almost disqualified before the start. She tried to unseat her jockey on the way out. She refused to enter the stalls. She wasted time and the Starter looked at his watch.

Mo shouted from the rails,

'Lady! Stop messin' about, or you'll get what for!'

The filly stopped prancing and kicking and trotted forward into the stalls without complaint, as if she heard the command. The jockey gave Mo a thankful wave and then they were off.

Charles Burton watched from the Stand. His wife held his arm and willed the Lady to win. Mike stood with them, anxiously looking through his binoculars.

The Lady was last to break from the stalls, from an unfavourable draw, and was trailing along at the back at the halfway point.

There seemed to be no hope of her catching the leaders.

Anna Burton squeezed her husband's hand. Mike was steeling himself for another defeat, already preparing his excuses, when The Lady moved up through the field, bringing them back to her one by one.

As they rounded the final bend with Dangerous Lady third, Charles Burton began to shout with excitement.

'Come on, Lady! Come on!'

Mike felt a thrill at the turn of speed The Lady showed, as if in response. Maybe he was right. This horse could be the one . . .

Dangerous Lady accelerated past the second horse and was upsides with the leader in the final furlong.

'Come on, come on!'

She continued to find more speed, overtook the favourite and was on the bridle as she met the winning post over a length ahead, still pulling.

Anna Burton danced ecstatically. Charles Burton hugged her, his face shining with delight. When they looked round, Mike had gone.

*

Jack Ross saw the race on television, from his wheelchair.

'Not bad! First and second, from two starts!'

Frances got up from the sofa to pour him another beer.

'James Brant wouldn't agree . . .'

Jack looked scornful and waved aside the beer.

'There's pop in the fridge. Let's do it some damage.'

Frances looked thoughtful when she brought the champagne, which Jack insisted on opening. He poured them a tulip glass each.

'To Arkenfield!'

Frances raised hers in acknowledgement.

'Dad, what happened?'

'Hmm?'

'There's a photograph on Mike's desk. His wife and son . . .'

'I thought you knew . . . ?'

'I wasn't here, was I?'

Jack lowered his eyes and stared at the bubbles.

The Arkenfield yard celebrated victory. When the horsebox arrived back, Charles Burton was there with his wife to meet it. He thanked everyone with particular grace and gave Joe, as Head Lad, two fifty-pound notes.

'Tonight, the party's on me,' he announced.

'Thanks, Mr Burton, sir,' said Joe, pocketing the money quickly, before Mike spotted it. He was too late.

'A drink would've been enough,' said Mike, disapprovingly.

But Burton was filled with good humour.

'The money doesn't matter, Mike.' He drew his wife to him, curling his arm round her shoulders. 'The horse . . . Today . . .'

He kissed Anna gently on the forehead.

'To me, they're beyond price . . .'

Anna smiled, with filling eyes.

Mike turned away. A sudden pain had stabbed him: the memory of Sally kissing him with that tenderness, once.

He was glad of the noisy diversion as Mo was carried on Nick's shoulders towards the heap of stable spoil, screaming, followed by the lads.

'Gerroff! Gerroff!'

Burton roared with laughter as Mo was tossed into the deepest part of it.

Rosie Carson glanced at her messages, as Mike searched the office for something he missed. Her reorganization irritated him.

'Sir Anthony Maybank rang. Would you call back?'

'Never heard of him.'

'He saw the race. He has two horses. Looking for a new trainer.'

'Oh?'

Mike tried to sound casual, but his eyes lit up. Rosie ticked her list without expression.

'Miss Ross rang. She's booked a table to celebrate at the Oast House. Could you pick her up at eight thirty? If you're not otherwise engaged . . .'

'Anyone else?'

'Mr Brant. Would you go to his house? He sounded cross. What are you looking for?'

'Oh, er – '

'The toy train is in the left-hand filing cabinet – under M for miscellaneous.'

Mike opened the drawer and picked out the tiny Mallard steam locomotive he had kept from his childhood. He had given it to his son.

Sally left it behind, to make a point, he thought, but what point?

He put it back where it belonged on the shelf, daring Rosie to move it again.

James Brant was more than cross. He roamed up and down the drawing room. He had made a mistake. He had seen Mike with Charles Burton at the races, enjoying their winner. He felt slighted and overlooked. Mike had taken advantage of him. He had looked foolish in front of his guests and Mike had offered neither explanation nor apology. His wife had given him little support. It was time to show his authority.

Mike seemed unrepentant.

'You've had every opportunity, Mike. I've backed you, stayed out of your way . . . What have I got to show?'

'Winners will come,' said Mike.

'Quicker for some,' Brant retorted.

'The Lady's a gift. She can put Arkenfield on the map.'

'Sorry. My mind's made up.' He looked at Kath, who avoided his eyes. 'Either you agree to go private, get rid of your other horses, or I withdraw my backing and find another trainer.'

Mike said nothing.

Kath was disgusted, but she knew better than to argue with her husband in this mood.

'Think. Give me your answer on Monday,' said Brant, by way of dismissal.

Mike was preoccupied throughout the meal in the Oast House. Frances tried to encourage him to talk.

'You've already decided, haven't you?'

'If the Lady wins a few more, I'll be turning owners away.'

She stressed the risk, but Mike had tasted triumph. His winner had opened up possibilities. Charles Burton was the sort of owner he wanted, not James Brant. Mike had no intention of being a Permit trainer, working for one owner. He held a Public Licence, part of the original agreement. He was not going back. Brant knew nothing about horses. The finest trainer in the world couldn't make winners of his rags.

He put his hand on hers.

'I believe in doing things while you can, that's all.'

Frances kept her hand on the table, not moving.

The Dog was in uproar. Joe had handed the landlord the money he got from Charles Burton, with instructions.

'Let me know when it's spent.'

The lads waded in, ordering pints. Mo drank cider with blackcurrant. Toasts were made all round, to Dangerous Lady and her owner, to Arkenfield, to the Jockey Club, to the great Eclipse, to Weatherby's, to Mike Hardy and Rosie the Dragon.

A policeman in uniform spoke to the landlord.

Nick pointed and made a joke about him searching for Mo, whose motor bike was untaxed and unroadworthy.

Mo looked suddenly fearful. She sprang up, ran to the ladies' and stayed there.

'Hey, it was a joke,' Nick said to the others. Danny watched the policeman leave, with a packet of crisps and a Scotch egg. He sipped his beer, thoughtfully, with a sly smile.

*

Jack Ross sat in darkness, looking out of the window at his moonlit front garden. He saw the headlights approach.

Mike got out of the new Land-Rover outside the house, walked round and opened the passenger door for Frances.

She stood very close.

For a moment, they were almost touching. Mike leaned forward to kiss her.

'No, Mike.' Frances turned away.

He tried again.

'Please don't,' she said, quietly. 'It's not you – the timing is all wrong.'

'Tonight was a real pleasure for me, Frances. I haven't been out for dinner with anyone for two years . . .'

'There was someone in America . . .'

'I guessed as much.'

'Oh?'

'The bruises show.'

'Only if you know where to look. Sorry, Mike. It's all too soon.'

'All right,' said Mike, touching her cheek gently. 'But I don't give up easily . . .'

She smiled and gave him a little wave as he got back into the Land-Rover and waited by the gate as he started the engine and drove off to Arkenfield.

Jack watched his daughter walk up the path.

Joe hurried across the yard towards the office, after Second Lot on Monday morning. He could see Mike through the window, talking on the telephone, looking very serious.

The lads were still hung-over. Joe dreaded telling them their weekend celebrations were for nothing.

He went into the office as Mike put the telephone down.

'You told him?'

'Yes. It'll take about two weeks for the legal side. That gives me time to find a new backer.'

Joe groaned, feeling worse. New backers for what? Yards were closing all around, in the recession. He saw unemployment facing them all, and he wondered how he would tell the staff.

Mike acted unconcerned.

'Mike O'Shea rang about Mo. He sacked her. Some trouble with the law. She attacked an owner'

'I know.'

'Since when?'

'Saturday night in the Dog. If you're thinking of giving her the push, it's hardly worth the bother now, is it?'

Before Mike could reply, there was a knock at the door. Mo came in, crying. She shuffled towards Mike's desk, with an open newspaper, hardly able to speak.

'Mo, what is it?'

'Something here in the paper . . .' she sobbed, suddenly.

Mike looked at the page. His face tightened in anguish as he read the headline and the brief report.

The church on the edge of the Downs was high and peaceful. Stone curlews called plaintively, answered by echoes, and peewits wheeled in flocks.

Mike stood alone near the lych-gate, as mourners filed away from the graveside. The service had been well attended, with people standing at the back. Pressmen were gathered in groups, watching for prey.

Anna Burton sought Mike, taking him aside to walk with her past an old yew tree, among the leaning headstones, away from the rest.

'He knew he was dying,' she said, without tears. 'His liver had long given up.'

Mike admired again her quiet courage.

'After the race, we went home, had dinner together. He was on top form. Charles at his best. Funny. Outrageous. Flirting. As if we were nineteen . . .'

She paused, looking at children playing.

'He went to his study, later on. Wanted to work, he said.'

Mike tried to understand her. She seemed quite calm.

'A cocktail of Scotch and pills did it. The coroner gave him the benefit of the doubt, but I knew . . .'

'But why then? He was on such a high . . .'

'At Westminster – you know what they called him? The Master of Mistiming. When he was close to an appointment, something always went wrong. That's why he took to the bottle – and the horses.'

'I had no idea . . .'

'In a way, that race was one of his greatest moments. His timing was perfect, for once. He didn't want to die by inches . . .'

She rested her hand on his arm.

'He went out a winner. Thanks to you and The Lady.'

They walked slowly back, towards the lines of cars. Mike had an uncomfortable feeling that she wanted to say something else. It seemed a long time before she did.

'What with one thing and another, Charles left rather a lot of debts . . . More than I can cover . . .'

Mike knew immediately, before she said it.

'I'm afraid The Lady will have to go . . .'

Mo cantered across the skyline on Dangerous Lady, then turned. Mike and Frances watched, standing by the Land-Rover, as she started her gallop.

'A hundred thousand, at least,' said Frances.

'About what I figured.'

'There's some interest.'

'Arabs?'

'No, French. What about your other owners?'

'I rang around,' said Mike, in a weary voice. 'They couldn't raise that between them.'

Frances tried to lift his spirits.

'Thanks, by the way.'

'For what?'

'Behaving like a gentleman.'

She squeezed his hand, encouragingly. Mike did not respond. He opened the door of the Land-Rover for her. She paused, before getting in.

'Mike?'

He looked at her.

'Don't stop trying,' she said simply.

During the week before the Sales, secret networking began in earnest. Frances alerted Rachael, who drew up a list, then a shorter list. John Grey listened to their plans and spoke to others. Potential investors were approached to take a stake in Arkenfield, or Dangerous Lady, or both. Deals were struck, cancelled, re-struck and re-cancelled. Figures were looked at and passed to accountants to look at again. Dreams were discussed. Imaginary winners were ridden to glory over drinks and canapés, with cautious moneyed people, who looked for a high rate of return on capital with guaranteed profits . . .

Most of it came to nothing.

Mike dressed his best, in his only suit, and prepared to bid. Frances sat with him, listening to the auctioneer. Above them, prices flickered in four currencies, as bids were made. All manner of horses came under the hammer, with all manner of futures ahead of them.

Mo paraded Dangerous Lady around the inspection ring, fiercely staring ahead, avoiding all eyes. The Lady was well-behaved and gleaming, with patterns on her quarters, holding her head high. Catalogues were marked by critical viewers, who knew of her recent win and the sad death of her owner. The widow may not insist on a high reserve . . .

Mo offered Joe the reins, when The Lady's number was called to enter the selling ring. Joe shook his head.

'You do it, Mo. It's only right.'

Hugo Latimer sat in his accustomed spot, bidding to order. He was well known to the auctioneer and his blink was a bid.

The price rose rapidly from twenty to eighty thousand guineas, with Hugo topping every bid from the floor. There was a short pause.

John Grey spotted James Brant standing by the aisle and gave Mike a nudge.

Dangerous Lady trotted in circles, Mo holding her without effort.

At ninety thousand there was another pause.

The auctioneer looked around and asked for more.

In the silence, Mike looked at Frances, who nodded.

'Ninety-two,' said Mike, in a clear voice.

Hugo countered with ninety-five.

They passed the psychological barrier of a hundred thousand. With no one else bidding, the price rose quickly to one hundred and fifteen thousand guineas. Hugo sat back in his seat, the bid with him.

'One twenty,' said Mike.

Hugo hesitated. The auctioneer waited a long moment, until Hugo finally shook his head.

The auctioneer was satisfied and called the sale twice. Frances held on to Mike's arm.

'One twenty-five,' a new bidder shouted from the aisle.

It was James Brant.

Kath Brant strolled through the buyers outside, with Rachael, glancing at yearlings with all hope before them and knobby-kneed foals penned-in, some still unweaned, all scrutinized endlessly, with much feeling of legs. Kath spotted Joe coming out of the selling ring.

'Seen my husband?'

Joe looked at her, warily.

'Inside – bidding against the Guv'nor. Price through the roof,' he said, hurrying away.

Kath looked at Rachael in sudden horror.

'Oh, no – '

They ran to the selling ring.

Joe watched Danny talking to two police officers in uniform, one male, one female, by a chequered patrol car near the entrance. He was pointing to the selling ring and talking animatedly. Joe didn't need to hear what he was saying.

'Bloody little bastard!' he swore, retracing his steps.

The bid stood at one thirty-five, with Brant. Mike rubbed his neck and looked at Frances and John Grey. They both nodded.

'One forty,' he called out, nervously.

Across the ring, he could see Kath talking to her husband passionately. The auctioneer looked to Brant, waiting for his response. Brant slumped, shaking his head.

'One hundred and forty thousand guineas, once, twice . . .'

The gavel dropped.

Mo jumped with delight. Frances hugged John Grey. Mike stared at the ground between his legs, holding his shaking knees.

'We did it! We did it!' Mo chanted, in the ring.

Then she saw the two police officers, standing by the doors. She thrust The Lady's reins into Joe's hands, and ran.

She scrambled over the edge of the ring and up through the serried seats, followed by the officers. They caught her before she could break through the crowd. Mike tried to intervene.

'She works for me. What's going on?'

Before the policeman could catch his breath, Mo knee-capped him with her jodhpurs boot. The WPC held her in an arm-lock.

'Get her in the car!'

Mo was marched away by the woman police officer, firmly held.

'Maureen Alice Ratcliffe is in breach of a probation order. She's bloody-well nicked,' said the policeman to Mike, as he hobbled after them.

James Brant looked deflated in front of his wife. Mike was nonplussed, searching for answers beyond him. The two men tried not to look at each other.

Mike said, 'I don't understand . . . I was already way over my limit . . .'

'I guessed you'd put something together, some syndicate, to buy The Lady . . .'

'Rachael called me,' said Kath. 'Didn't you, Rachael?'

'Kath told me you intended to out-bid Mike.'

Both men looked sheepish.

'What I didn't know,' said Brant to Rachael, 'was that you were half of it.'

'Kath agreed to take the other half over lunch.'

'On condition that yours was the final bid.'

Realization slowly dawned on them.

After Hugo had bailed out at a hundred and fifteen thousand guineas, they had been bidding against themselves.

'So I own half a horse. Who owns the rest?'

'I split my half into two. A quarter to me. A quarter between the rest.'

'John Grey has fifteen per cent, Frances five. Joe and I scratched around for the other five,' Mike said, ruefully.

Kath looked at her husband, with a faint smile.

'Don't you think you can both start behaving like grown-ups?'

Brant said nothing. Mike turned away. Rachael and Kath pretended not to be interested.

Eventually, Brant coughed and said, 'I suppose I could call a halt to the winding-up process . . .'

'On one condition,' Mike put in, quickly.

The two women groaned in unison.

'What?' Brant wanted to know, giving nothing away.

'Mo Ratcliffe. We need her. If The Lady's going to do anything . . .'

THREE

Mo Ratcliffe ran down the steps of the Magistrates Court.

The hearing was over. She had spent the night in a police cell. She felt angry, dirty and petulantly defiant. She wanted to lash out at someone, or get away.

Mike followed her, shouting.

'Hey!'

'What?'

'Come back here!'

Mo stopped, briefly, without looking back.

'I've said ta. I'm leaving. I've left.'

Mike caught up with her and tried to lead her to the car-park in front of the building.

'This way.'

'Gerroff!'

She pulled away from him. Mike's voice hardened and he turned to climb back up the steps.

'Right. I'll go back inside and tell 'em I'm *not* responsible. Start running.'

Mo hesitated. Mike did not stop, and she was forced to run up after him.

'Sorry,' she said, changing her tone.

Mike ignored her and reached for the doors.

'Very sorry. I'm dead grateful you spoke up for me. But you don't have to keep me on.'

Mike left a long pause, before relenting.

'Finished?'

'Yes.'

Mike turned to face her.

'Then remember one thing. No more thumping owners, like the one in Ireland. Not my owners.'

Mo's eyes suddenly shone with hope.

'You mean—?'

He led her down the steps before saying, quietly: 'You've done a year or so of your apprenticeship. I'm going to give you a chance to finish it. Get in.'

He pointed to the silver Arkenfield Land-Rover.

Mo was stunned. Then her face split in a huge grin of delight.

Tom Fisher, Mike's solicitor, had a bad day at the races.

On his fiftieth birthday, be became the owner of a racehorse, a present from his giddy wife, Paula. A grey two-year-old colt called Chieftain's Son, by Border Chief out of Misha Moo. A nice animal, with a short, sharp action and a frisky nature.

Tom Fisher was a racegoer and a gambler. He had no interest in owning a horse, but he put it in training with Mike, in the hope of mutual favours, business for business.

Chieftain's Son was a better horse than anyone expected. Paula had picked up an amazing bargain, with no knowledge at all, in her scatter-brained way. She thought he was 'pretty'.

The grey showed speed. Tom Fisher decided it would make the frame on its first run, so he placed a large each-way bet to get his 'good touch' and counted on a profit.

Chieftain's Son was second in a photo-finish.

But Tom Fisher was angry. Paula irritated him by gushing in front of the Weighing Room, Mike disappointed him by not turning up to the meeting, but what infuriated him was the price.

'Training and racing aren't the same thing . . .' said Mike, as if that explained it.

Tom Fisher stood in the yard, watching the grey being unloaded from the box. Joe, Danny and Nick were sharing the work, taking off the tail bandage, knee boots and travelling bandage, as the other horses peered nosily out, snorting and talking amongst themselves.

Mike had just arrived back from court with Mo.

'I pay for the racing,' said Tom Fisher, emphatically, turning his back on the horse and going towards the office.

Mike heard Nick's brief account of the race. Then he followed the solicitor into the Arkenfield office, preparing excuses.

'Damn near won,' he said, rubbing his hands. 'Would've done, if Ronnie Foulkes hadn't been a pound over. A pound is a neck, at that distance.'

Tom Fisher was not interested in the jockey's weight.

'That's not the point,' he said, coldly.

Mike caught on immediately.

'You didn't make money . . .'

'I lost money.'

'I don't set the price,' Mike shrugged. 'The on-course bookies do.'

Tom Fisher was scathing.

'First time out at five to four . . .?'

Mike had no explanation for the keen starting price.

'I didn't back it,' he said with his hands up.

'You weren't there. Which is another thing.'

'I had an important—'

Tom Fisher cut him off before he could explain about the court hearing.

'I'm not accusing you, Mike,' Tom Fisher said, looking out of the window. 'You have a stable leak . . .'

Chieftain's Son trotted round. The lads were shouting to one another. Rosie the Dragon was typing.

'A stable leak?'

'Yes.'

Mike was taken aback.

'Someone in your yard is handing out information. I want to take my horse away, Mike . . . I think you'll find other owners will, too . . .'

Rosie Carson brought out Tom Fisher's account, as Mike played for time.

Information?

There were unwritten rules. The difficulty of picking a winner beforehand is eased a little by an industry of information-mongers, predicting the unpredictable. Inside information about a horse's health and fitness is commonly printed in racing newspapers. But *valuable* information . . .

'You're paid up to date,' Mike said, briskly.

'Any odds and ends – let me know.'

'If you're that unhappy, Tom . . .'

Mike tried to be business-like. He was not going to plead with Tom Fisher.

'We're not all James Brant,' said Fisher. 'I'm not rich. Five to four, first time out, says it all. I imagine all your owners will be wondering.'

'My staff are loyal. To me,' said Mike, fiercely.

Tom Fisher raised an eyebrow. 'In a new venture? Really? There's no history . . .'

'I stand by them.'

67

Mike was firm. Rosie the Dragon stopped typing.

Tom Fisher looked at him, coolly, for a moment. Then he seemed to change his mind.

'Let's leave it for a month. No training fees. Where are we now?'

He took his eyes away from Mike and looked at the date panel on his watch.

'No training fees?'

The solicitor paused and looked up.

'I'm trying to help you,' he said, as Mike winced. 'Meantime, check your security, your staff, everyone . . .'

Mo and Danny were letting down Chieftain's Son in his box, working on either side of the horse. Mo was singing with happiness and countered Danny's sly questions cheerfully.

'Probation?' he asked.

'If you must know.'

'No, tell me. I can help, maybe.'

'Yeah.'

Mo ignored his false sympathy and brushed steadily.

'Hitting owners . . .?'

'And robbin' banks. Got millions stashed.' Mo was enjoying it.

'I can find out.'

Danny sounded nasty again. She preferred that.

'Spread it round. Stick it in the paper. While you're at it, you can tell 'em I'm now Arkenfield's apprentice jock. Ho-fficial.'

Danny stopped working.

'You?'

'Finishing off. I've done a year.'

'What about me?'

Mo looked at him, as if surprised by the question. Danny's face suddenly twisted.

'Hey, bloody Nora!'

A shadow darkened the half-door. Mike's voice rang out.

'You two!'

'That right, Guv'nor? Is she bein' made up apprentice?'

'Office. Sharpish.'

The staff gathered in Mike's office, waiting for him to speak. He looked out of the window into the yard, with his back facing them. Rosie sat at her desk. Tom Fisher had gone. Danny felt only resentment as he stood next to Mo. Nick and Joe were on either side of Mike's desk.

They looked at each other in the long silence.

Mike turned and glared.

'Which one of you is on the take?'

They were shocked: then offended. His words were too blunt. Joe Hogan, the eldest and most experienced, spoke carefully.

'You mean the price today? Chieftain's Son at five to four?'

Mike looked hard into their eyes, in turn.

'Danny?'

'Me?' Danny's voice was scornful and shrill.

'What are we being accused of?' Nick wanted to know. 'Selling information to bookies?'

'Who? Me?'

They were outraged. Mike changed his tone.

'I'm talking about loyalty. This yard is straight.'

'Hey, Guv'nor. Hold on,' Joe said, wounded.

'I'm straight. I don't want anyone here who isn't,' said Mike.

'You mean I'm not?' Danny challenged.

'One of you, at least.'

'Why one of us?'

'I'm not being bloody accused,' said Joe, angrily turning to leave.

'Could be anyone,' Danny pressed. 'An owner, or Brant, even . . .'

'Joe, I didn't say you could leave,' Mike called out, sharply.

'Couldn't bloody care less,' Joe growled, banging the door after him.

Mike hadn't intended this: his words had been badly chosen. He turned to Rosie for support. She did not look sympathetic.

'Whoever it is, it's not me,' said Rosie, coldly.

'Me neither,' said Danny, starting a chorus.

Mike turned back to the window in dismissal, furious with himself at his bad man-management.

'You can all get out,' he said. 'But one of you knows what I'm talking about . . .'

Kath Brant heard Mike's voice in the hall. The housekeeper was protesting. She put down her watercolour brush.

Their house was her domain. She resisted her husband's grosser attempts to climb non-existent ladders.

She liked Mike, even though he trained horses.

'He is in, but I don't think he wants to be disturbed,' she said, overruling Alice.

'Shame,' said Mike grimly.

'He's been on the telephone for hours. Something to do with European Community funding . . .'

Mike walked purposefully down the hall, towards Brant's study.

'I really wouldn't go in . . .' said Kath, lamely.

*

James Brant was in full flow.

'Both consultants made the right noises. They're all at the trough, with their bloody up-front fees. Professionals are taking over. We were given clear indications . . . Of course not. The whole thing isn't viable, on a commercial basis. Everyone knows that.'

He looked up to see Mike standing in front of him.

'I want to see you,' said Mike.

'Sod off.'

'No.'

Brant swung round in his chair, ignoring him. He continued his conversation, growing more concerned as he listened.

Mike waited.

'Write to Charles,' said Brant, vehemently. 'Yes, that Charles.'

He slammed the phone down. For a moment, he sat rigidly, lost in battle.

Mike spoke.

'Do you know anything about a stable leak?'

'What?'

'I want to know what you know about it.'

Brant stared at him. It could have been a voice from another world.

'I'm talking about thirty-five million pounds,' he said. 'What the hell are you talking about?'

Mike's problem shrivelled. He had charged in again.

'Sorry, James,' he said, genuinely.

Despite himself, Brant was disarmed. He revealed his inner nature by taking a deep breath and pointing towards a decanter.

'I'm supposed to be converting a cotton mill into an arts

71

centre with craft workshops. It has no basis in reality. What's your problem?'

Mike poured Brant an amontillado.

'Someone's been giving information affecting the betting,' he said, pointedly avoiding pouring a drink for himself, 'and I thought of you.'

Brant sipped his sherry.

'Have you said anything?'

'About betting?'

'About horses.'

Brant sighed and said, feelingly, 'If I had my way – I'd do nothing else.'

'My owners have complained. If they take their horses away—'

'Well, let them. I warned you.'

Brant picked up the telephone again. It was a dismissal.

'I've got to ring Brussels,' he said, entering a number. 'But I will say this. Someone in Europe with a very big mouth has been talking about my project. It's the same game . . . You find 'em and jump on 'em.'

Mike backed away, defeated.

'I will.'

'You know what you'll discover?'

'What?'

'It's usually one of your friends,' said Brant, as the number answered.

Mike left the study, listening to Brant's changed voice, booming.

'Oh, hallo, George. Jim here. Absolutely fine . . .'

He walked out into the hall, where Kath was hovering. She looked at him, kindly.

'Well?'

'I'm better with horses,' said Mike, flatly, walking to the door.

Jack Ross shouted up the stairs.

'Frances!'

'Down in a minute!'

'Come in,' he said to Mike.

Mike followed him into the sitting room.

'Is it that bad?'

'Eh?'

'Don't *you* get visitors?'

'Me?' Jack laughed, sarcastically. 'Oh, they're never off the doorstep.'

Mike sat down. He had arranged to take Frances to the Dog.

'Well, I wouldn't mind a word.'

'About that rag you've got?'

'What rag?'

'Chieftain's Son. The price. I saw the race.'

'Did you back it?'

'More sense. Somebody did.'

'That's what I wanted a word about.'

'You'll have to learn to keep your mouth shut,' Jack said, as Frances came down the stairs.

'Me?'

Jack eased himself into his wheelchair, affecting more pain than he felt, and grumbled, 'I suppose you're both going out now . . . ?'

When they arrived at the Dog, Frances complained to Mike about her father.

'He gets worse.'

'No. He always was an awkward sod.'

'I worry about him . . . Not about whether he rides again. I don't think he will . . .'

Mike sensed that she was concealing her real thoughts and sipped his orange juice.

'If he doesn't . . .?'

'You don't understand. I didn't expect to *be* here.'

Frances wanted to talk about her life in Kentucky and the freedom she felt there. Mike did not have the responsibility of being the only child of an only parent. She wanted to tell someone about her love affair and how it had damaged a part of her in a way she couldn't explain. Mike was a friend. She had known him for most of her life. Yet they knew very little about each other.

'You want to tell me?' Mike asked, gently.

For a moment, she considered it.

But John Grey came in and spotted them. The moment passed. New drinks were ordered, new topics discussed.

'Hey, what happened to your horse today?' John Grey enquired.

'Ronnie Foulkes on the beer. A pound over.'

'I meant the price.'

Mo Ratcliffe stood alone in the Arkenfield yard, her face golden in the evening sunset. She smiled at the sky and the racehorse-shaped weather-vane on the roof in rapture, arms outstretched, embracing the ethos of the old stable.

She twirled slowly, making the place her own in a way no home had been in her life. She felt mysterious radiations from the walls and boxes, as if ghosts of winners still lived. It was a private act of communion and dedication.

Then, with a whoop of joy, she ran round and round the circular wooden tack-room in the middle of the yard.

*

Early-doors regulars in the Dog and Gun were used to strangers later in the evening crowding into the small dining area, off the main bar.

John Grey touched Mike on the sleeve.

'There's John Pilgrim, for instance.'

He indicated a man in his mid-fifties, eating a steak, with a cigarette burning in the ashtray in front of him.

Mike knew the name and dismissed it at once.

'He's got shops. Wouldn't be him.'

'Sold his shops to the Firms. On-course only now.'

Mike lifted an eyebrow. He looked across at John Pilgrim, a bookmaker. John Pilgrim & Son had been founded in 1950. Mike's father had bet there. Mike remembered the motto: 'Pilgrim Always Pays'.

The man eating was Son. Opposite him, his wife Brenda sat with their son, another of the same name, known as Jackie. They were infrequent regulars, who drove out from Newbury, for the large portions of good homely food and low prices. John Pilgrim was famous for his irascibility.

'Must be well loaded,' Mike said, without interest.

John Grey pursued the thought in his mind.

'Small bookies – they didn't all sell willingly. Some got squeezed out. Then Capital Gains . . .'

'I'm bleeding.'

'Last of a line, though. Father a bookie – John Pilgrim as well – dead a long time – but the son . . .'

John Grey grimaced.

'What's wrong with him?' Frances asked, looking at Jackie, a blue-eyed, rugged, black-haired man in his twenties.

'You tell me. Had every opportunity.'

'Probably why,' Mike retorted.

John Grey continued to look at the Pilgrims, as the conversation turned.

In the public bar games were played. The atmosphere was different. Here, stable lads threw darts and swilled pints. Strangers could not penetrate the secret local subculture and kept out.

Joe Hogan reigned every night.

Drinking and talking, laughing and joking, smoke thick on the ceiling, lads and lasses from all the yards packed the room until closing time and beyond.

'In my day, an apprentice was a slave, nearly,' said Joe, celebrating Mo's promotion, for something to celebrate.

'I don't care what,' said Mo. 'It's a big chance.'

Mo was amazed to find herself suddenly popular: elevated in rank, she was now one of the aristocrats of the public bar, an apprentice jockey.

Danny continued to mock her at every opportunity.

'You'll get turned down, when they find out. They won't want you, with a criminal record.'

'Shut up, piggery.'

'I'm only saying—'

'Yes, they will,' said Joe, supporting her, 'with the right recommendations. She'll get all that.'

'No, they won't,' Danny persisted, 'Ask Nick.'

He turned to get Nick involved, but Nick wasn't there.

'Where is he? In the bog?'

He looked round. The passageway leading to the lavatories was common to both bars.

Jackie Pilgrim emerged from the gents' as two stable lads pushed their way in. He made his way back to the main bar and dining area.

Stevie the landlord strode through the rooms, ringing a handbell, chanting his familiar, singsong phrase,

'Peers, poets and peasants, last orders please.'

Jackie paused to say something briefly to Stevie before rejoining his parents at the table. Stevie's face clouded.

Jackie sat opposite his mother, Brenda. She had been beautiful, once. Now she was overweight. She pushed her plate across the table to her son and simpered, 'Oh, this cheesecake . . . I can't finish it. Go on, Jackie.'

'Have I got to?'

He knew he had no choice.

John Pilgrim lit a cigarette and looked at him.

'All right?' he asked.

Father and son exchanged a look, while Brenda smiled, indulgently, not knowing what it meant.

Jackie nodded, his mouth full of cheesecake.

The Dog was always busy in the last hour. The landlord made his way through the customers to the toilets, as two stable lads came out.

He went inside. There was no one in sight. He was about to leave, when he heard a groan coming from an open cubicle.

He approached, cautiously and looked in.

A figure knelt on the floor, hunched over the bowl retching.

'You all right, lad?'

Nick turned round. One eye was closing. Blood ran from his lip, where a tooth was smashed. Broken skin on his nose showed raw flesh. He looked a mess.

'Yeah, fine. Great.'

FOUR

Jackie Pilgrim helped his mother on with her coat.

The bar was busy. Everyone clamoured for the last round. John Pilgrim paid the bill from a roll of notes big enough to choke a cow.

'Good as always,' he said to the waitress, giving her a few pound coins. 'Put those in your pot.'

They were ready to leave.

John Pilgrim lit another cigarette as they pushed slowly through to the main bar, nodding good-nights. Brenda smiled vaguely to everyone.

'Mr Pilgrim, leaving before the last race?' John Grey said, as they passed.

Pilgrim peered sourly at him, recognizing him immediately. Spotting 'faces' in a crowd was a vital part of his trade. He grunted, which was his usual way of greeting people he didn't want to know.

'This is Frances Ross, Jack Ross's daughter, now "stock agent", and Mike Hardy, trainer. John Pilgrim.'

Pilgrim grunted again.

'All in the horse trade, Mr Pilgrim,' John Grey said in a cheerful, friendly voice Mike knew to be false.

Pilgrim coughed, and pushed past.

'I'm a bookie. What do I know about bloody horses?'

John Grey smiled when he'd gone. He seemed pleased

with himself and tried to catch the eye of a barmaid for the last drink.

'Not for me,' said Frances, 'I have to rush off. Dad still thinks I'm about twelve.'

Just before leaving, Mike had a last word with Grey, whispering,

'See what you can find out . . .'

'I will.'

Mike followed Frances to the door.

John Grey ordered a 'domestic' – a large gin, with ice and bitters – and wandered through to the public bar, where he was always accepted.

Nick splashed his face with cold water. The landlord examined him carefully.

'Bastard,' said Nick, spitting, 'landed me when I wasn't lookin' – I don't know what with. Wasn't a fist.'

'Who was it?'

'Don't ask, Stevie.'

'I've got to ask. Licensed premises. If you want to fight, you go outside.'

'It wasn't a fight. Don't make a big deal.'

The landlord had years of experience.

'Well, I don't think you need a doctor. A dentist, maybe.'

Danny burst in. Nick was too late to hide his face.

'We thought you'd died,' said Danny. Then he saw Nick's face.

'Somebody hit him,' Stevie said, levelly.

'Who?'

'Just make sure the guv'nor doesn't find out,' Nick commanded, ignoring the question.

Danny was known for his boxing, in the Lads' championship.

'Tell me who – I'll sort 'em.'

'I'll do any sorting,' said Nick, harshly.

The landlord spoke sharply to two stable lads and asked them to leave. They protested. Jeers rose in the public bar, as lads from rival yards took sides. Stevie handled it well; he was always fair. The noise increased. Danny weaved and threatened, Joe argued, Mo shouted and Nick slipped quietly out of the back door of the pub, unnoticed. John Grey sat at the domino table and drinks were served after time.

Another good night in the Dog.

When Jack Ross heard Frances come in, he switched off the television. He tried not to wait up for her as he knew she hated it. He permitted her every freedom, he thought. He was careful not to question her.

Mike followed her into the sitting room.

'I thought you'd be in bed,' Frances said, sharply.

'Just going up . . .'

'I've asked Mike in for coffee.'

'Oh,' said Jack, not moving from his wheelchair. 'In that case, I wouldn't say no . . . I'd like a word with Mike.'

Frances glared at her father for a second, then flounced into the kitchen to put the kettle on.

Jack struggled to his feet, opened a corner cupboard and brought out a bottle of whisky.

'Still off it?'

'Yes.'

Jack nodded and poured himself a large measure. They could hear Frances banging crockery.

'I didn't want her to come back from America,' Jack

explained. 'She insisted. Had everything going for her there . . .'

Mike sat down, feeling uncomfortable.

'Talk of marriage . . .'

Mike avoided his eyes, trying to seem unaffected.

'Mind you, a right bastard, he is,' said Jack, viciously.

'It's none of my business, Jack.'

Mike was conscious of Frances moving about and wondered if she could hear. He felt like an intruder.

'Oh, isn't it?'

'No,' Mike replied, too quickly.

'Look, you've taken a beating as well. Sally gone. A lad you can't see . . . I'm just trying to avoid more pain.'

Mike stood up, annoyed.

'Where are you going?'

'Home,' he said.

Frances appeared in the doorway, with a tray. Mike looked from father to daughter. Jack tried to save the moment and justify himself.

'I was only saying I don't want to keep you here. I want you to go back to America. When I get over this . . .'

'I'm not going back,' Frances snapped, angrily.

'That bastard messing you about – '

'Dad, will you shut up? Shut up!' She slammed the tray on the table.

Mike edged into the hall.

'Good-night, Frances . . .' he mumbled.

'Mike?'

She went after him. Mike opened the front door.

'Mike, for the record – marriage wasn't mentioned. I think you know who he's talking about . . .'

Mike did not know.

'. . . and he did mess me about.'

'Who?'

'David Ware.'

Mike drove back to Arkenfield, feeling sickened. He did not think he could feel pain on top of pain. He couldn't understand why the thought of David Ware and Frances making love hurt so much. She was only a friend.

He turned into the yard and stopped. Restraining himself from slamming the door, because of the horses, he walked slowly over to the security fence. He hung from his fingers knotted into the wire-mesh, staring into the yard for a long time, his face twisted and his mind dark.

Nick was the first customer in the Dog, soon after opening time the next morning. He apologized to the landlord for causing the disturbance and received a free pint.

'Guv'nor seen the face yet?' Stevie enquired.

'No. I'm keeping out of the way.'

The landlord was surprised when John Grey came in. Customers were rare in the first hour.

'Kicked by a horse, Nick?'

'Mr Grey – yeah.'

They did not believe it.

'Early for you,' the landlord commented, looking at John Grey.

'Actually it's quite late,' John Grey said, mysteriously, 'I think I'll try a pint.'

As Stevie pulled the hand-pump again, John Grey spoke quietly to Nick.

'I want to talk to you about a few horses . . .'

They moved to a corner, with their drinks, and talked in low voices. Stevie replenished stocks on the shelves and supervised the staff as the new day got under way. He glanced at them occasionally and saw Nick staring discon-solately at the floor.

'Who told you?' asked Nick, at length.

John Grey shrugged: what did it matter?

'I heard it twice. The sums were slightly different.'

'How much?'

'One said eight hundred pounds. The other said seven hundred and fifty.'

Nick felt sick. He thought nobody in the village knew.

'Which is it?'

'Both,' he said, 'I paid off fifty – '

John Grey remained calm.

'Not an awful lot of money, even on your wages. You've owed it for what, three years?'

'Before I was even at Latimer's.'

'So much a week . . . ?'

'Wouldn't let me.'

'All bookies will let you, if it's the only way. They can't enforce gambling debts. So why not?'

Nick looked uncomfortable.

'They wanted it all in one go, they said. I saved up a bit in the Post Office . . .'

'They wanted the information more than the money.'

'Of course. Just how they were running and that. Not much . . .'

'Quite valuable, to a bookie . . .'

Nick sounded bitter.

'Cost them nothing – and I still owe.'

John Grey finished his pint and reached for Nick's empty glass.

'Another?'

Nick nodded, miserably. John Grey seemed brighter.

'John Pilgrim had to sell the shops. To pay for Jackie's mismanagement. There isn't enough left for the tax-man.'

'Oh?'

John Grey stood up. It all fitted now, in his mind.

'Should be a trading loss, but no. Capital Gains. They're making him bankrupt.'

Nick felt lost. He did not understand, but it made a sort of sense.

'Jackie Pilgrim tried to get information out of me, once,' John Grey mused.

'You? What happened?'

'Oh, I gave it to him . . .'

He smiled blandly, as he went to the bar.

Rachael Ware swam in her pool, cleaving a neat crawl, end to end, flipping over at the turn. She swam regularly, to maintain her figure, which was still that of a girl.

David must go.

She hated Frank's son living in her house. She hated his untidiness, his beer-cans, his magazines, his presence at night, his insinuations, his body . . .

She saw him beside the pool, sprawled out, legs apart, almost naked; a trim, muscular twenty-five-year-old, sunning himself.

She hated the way he looked at her. She felt trapped, knowing she would have to climb out of the pool soon. She had left her towelling robe beside the sun-lounger where David now lay.

An hour ago, she had been alone.

Now, she would have to walk over there in her swimsuit, with his eyes on her. She was tired.

David had been offered a job with Hugo Latimer. Rachael hoped it would include accommodation. She wondered if David had bought himself the job with the money he made from Raw Silk.

She climbed out of the pool, dripping. She would have to say something. She wanted to do what was right, for Frank's sake, but she didn't know what to do. She wished he was still alive.

David's eyes were on her.

She walked quickly over to him.

'This job with Hugo—' she said briskly. 'Does it have somewhere to live?'

'I don't know. Why?'

'Because if it doesn't, I want you to find somewhere . . .'

'Oh?' He looked at her, lazily.

Rachael backtracked a little, swathing herself quickly in her robe.

'I'm not throwing you out, David. I just find it very difficult.'

He raised himself on one arm and looked at her.

'I can understand that.'

'Can you?'

'You're still a young woman . . .'

She was suddenly angry. How dare he look at her like that?

'Don't say another word, David. I want you out of here.'

'OK,' he smiled, gently.

'I mean it. Within a week.'

She turned and ran back to the house.

John Grey sat on a stool at the bar, toying with a ploughman's lunch. Mike stood next to him, eating a sandwich.

Nick had gone, before the lunch-time regulars could see him.

85

John Grey outlined the scheme he had called Mike out to hear.

'I suggest a trial. Full dress, clocks, starting stalls, posts, discs, pickled onions.'

'A trial?' said Mike, doubtfully. 'Aren't we a bit old-fashioned?'

'Old-fashioned?'

'You mean a *trial* trial?'

'Absolutely. Above board, fair and square, even stevens, two-horse race. A check on form at the distance.'

Mike looked at him, sceptically. He had expected more from John Grey.

'Chieftain's Son – and which horse?'

'One with a rating we know about.'

Mike remained unimpressed.

'OK. What will that prove?'

John Grey leant forward.

'I will tell you,' he said.

A battered five-year-old Mercedes-Benz 350SL stopped in the narrow lane off The Rudge. A string of racehorses blocked the road, leaving no room for the car to pass.

A grey was rearing and getting out of line.

Inside the car, John Pilgrim was about to blast the horn. He checked himself.

'That's Chieftain's Son,' said Jackie, rubbing the fogged windscreen.

They were returning, circuitously, from a game of golf which Jackie had won. John Pilgrim smoked and stared furiously at the horses.

There was no hurry.

Jackie's mind worked on a plan. He knew his father was against it. His father was an uneducated tyrant.

John Pilgrim resented his son. He was the cause of his present distress, and he thought he was useless.

They were both right.

John Pilgrim revved the engine, impatiently.

'We need – how much do you think we need? – we need a hundred thousand,' he said, with his hand hovering over the horn.

Jackie had firm ideas about positive thinking.

'We use our *assets*, Dad . . .'

'We've got none – we're facing bankruptcy. *I'm* facing bankruptcy.'

The engine roared as he stamped the accelerator in emphasis.

'A good name,' Jackie spelled out, slowly.

'That isn't going to pay the blasted Revenue!'

'An *asset*, Dad,' he repeated.

' "Pilgrim Always Pays" – your grandad's motto.'

'We always have,' Jackie said, as if this supported his idea.

'We need fifty thousand *now* – this month.'

'And another asset we have . . . Inside information . . .'

John Pilgrim hated the shiftless thought-pattern of his son's mind. He refused to listen.

'If you'd concentrate on the actual *business*, instead of trying your damn short cuts, we might—'

But Jackie wouldn't be stopped.

'All we need – *all* we need – is *one favourite* which won't win. Some very big names started off with that.'

John Pilgrim shouted at him in exasperation.

'Bookmaking's a job! You work at it! Apply your mind!'

His pent-up fury made him smack the horn.

The horses skittered and pranced in alarm.

He was immediately sorry, and sat shamefacedly, as the riders struggled to regain control, cursing him.

'Not a job I want to do,' Jackie said, knowing how much it hurt his father. 'Never have. I'm sorry, Dad.'

It was their whole insoluble problem.

Nick stood in a doorway in the corner of the yard, trying to summon his nerve.

Chieftain's Son looked out of his box, his neck restricted by the bars of a weaving frame to prevent him swinging from side to side in the boredom. He nodded peacefully at the flies. It was the quiet time of the afternoon. Everything was still.

He saw Mike come out of his office and walk across to the tack room in the middle of the yard.

'You've got to tell him,' Mo hissed, from behind him.

'I'm going to.'

Nick gambled, Mike drank. At Latimer's, both knew each other's weakness.

Nick had confided in Mo. He came back from the Dog and she saw his face. It all came out.

He wanted to be a trainer, so he started betting, to raise capital, knowing something of Hugo's occasional 'jobs'. He listened to every whisper and rumour. He placed his bets carefully. For months he won more than he lost. He placed bigger bets with John Pilgrim.

Before long, he was behind. He bet larger amounts to recoup his losses and lost.

He did not tell Mike that he was in debt.

'Well go on, then,' said Mo, pushing him.

Mike compared different sizes of weight-cloth. They each had pockets sewn in to contain slivers of lead. He tried them under the saddles, to see how they fitted, and chose one. He began packing lead into the pockets, judiciously feeling the added weight. He slid more lead in, until he was satisfied with the feel of it and tried it under the saddle he intended to use.

The contours of the saddle concealed the weight-cloth beneath to his satisfaction.

He was startled to hear a voice.

'Guv'nor . . .'

Mike whipped round, hiding what he was doing.

'What?'

He saw Nick, standing diffidently in the doorway.

'Nick, come in.'

Nick hesitated.

Mike's voice softened, remembering his earlier bluntness, which had gone badly wrong.

'Come on in. Shut the door.'

Mo watched Nick enter the circular tack-room. She saw the door close. A round wooden hut with a conical roof, standing incongruously in the middle of the yard, so that horses could trot round it on the lunge, she supposed.

She stared at it for five minutes, waiting for it to explode.

In the public bar of the Dog and Gun that night, a different Nick sat with the Arkenfield team.

He did not recount every word Mike had said to him.

'Had my head snapped off,' was his short explanation, but they could see he was brighter.

'You're still here,' Mo said, pleased.

'If you were caught putting money on in the old days, you were straight down the road,' Joe put in.

They all knew Joe's weakness.

'You put money on!'

'Where's it got me? I'm still chasing the first pound, at my age.'

'You've won your share, Joe.'

'Well where is it? Why am I riding around on an old push-bike when bookies have Mercs?'

They were back to normal, it seemed.

Mike forced himself to see Frances.

Twice during the day, they met briefly, by accident. She came to the yard and watched Mike lunging Chieftain's Son in the manège for a few minutes. He turned on his heel in the centre, keeping the triangle of control, with the lunge-line in one hand and the long whip in the other, as the grey circled, and was unable to break his concentration to talk to her. When he stopped, Frances was gone.

He bumped into her later in the village shop, buying groceries. They discussed Chieftain's Son.

'Running Thursday at Sandown,' Mike said, casually. 'Like to come?'

'Love to,' Frances replied. 'Could do well . . .'

'I may be wrong. I often am . . .'

'Yes . . .'

They scanned the shelves. Mike said nothing more until they were outside.

'See you later, perhaps, in the Dog?'

David Ware hated warm English beer. He drank chilled lager in bottles, but preferred cans. He occupied John Grey's favourite corner, ordered his seventh bottle from Stevie and poured it into a glass. He would rather drink straight from cans.

John Grey stood reading the *Life*. He looked cross about

something and fidgeted with the paper.

'I've been offered a job with Hugo Latimer,' David Ware said, as a conversation opener.

John Grey hardly looked up.

'Very suitable. I'd take it,' he said, showing no interest.

David Ware thought about Rachael. Time was on his side. If she wanted him to move out, he would. Hugo had said he could have Mike's old rooms over the stable block. It was not far from the Ware Stud. He could plan his next moves in privacy, without her watching.

John Pilgrim did not like pubs. He was not sociable and would rather drink wine at home, where he would not have to speak. But he sat in the Dog and ordered a brandy, because Jackie had some urgent business there. He glared at anyone who showed signs of friendliness. The trouble with pubs was that people talked and asked questions he could not answer. Jackie had disappeared to the lavatory, leaving him alone. He chain-smoked and dreaded somebody speaking to him.

Mike followed Frances into the bar and greeted John Grey.

'Not in your usual spot?'

'Mike, Frances. What can I get you?' Too late, Mike saw David Ware. Frances was trapped between them.

'Hi, Frances. You're looking good,' David Ware said.

She looked at him, venomously, for a second. David smiled, but his eyes lost contact with hers. Mike moved round to stand between them, with his back to David Ware.

'White wine and soda for me, John,' Frances said, brightly.

'Mike?'

Mike turned to look at David Ware.

'You know my poison by now,' he said.

David Ware swallowed the last of his lager and forced a harsh laugh.

'Well, gotta go,' he said, as if reluctantly, heading for the door.

Jackie Pilgrim shoved Nick into the wall. Nick was scared of another beating.

'I'll get it, Jackie. I've said.'

'Good. What else have you got?'

'Well that's it, nothin'. They know.'

'Who knows?'

'The guv'nor. That's what I wanted to tell you. I daren't risk it any more, Jackie. You'll get the cash, somehow . . .'

Jackie Pilgrim drew his arm back. His hand held something solid.

'No, listen! There's a trial in the mornin' . . . Nine o'clock . . .'

'Tell me the result.'

'I can't, Jackie. But you can be there. Why not? Public right of way . . .'

Jackie Pilgrim was about to slam Nick in the face, when he heard the outer door of the gents' open.

Danny came in.

'OK, Nick?' he asked, looking suspicious.

'Yeah.'

Jackie Pilgrim glanced at himself in the mirror. He flicked his hair and went back to the bar to rejoin his father.

The Mercedes bumped along The Rudge and stopped. John Pilgrim got out and lit a cigarette. Jackie brought their binoculars. They settled on a vantage point hidden by blackthorn, from where they could view the vast open sea of Roden Down.

Far below, they could see a grey horse and a brown horse, surrounded by a small group of people.

They focused on the trial.

Twin practice starting stalls were set up. Danny operated the mechanical lever which released the horses. Joe acted as Starter. White markers discs were laid out in a line. Mike stood at the finish-point with a stop-watch.

Tom Fisher, in the three-piece suit he wore to the office, discussed the cost of ownership with James Brant. He was touting, but Brant ignored him.

Frances thought the trial was a public relations exercise for the benefit of awkward owners. A show for those who knew nothing about training, but paid the bills. She helped Mike by talking incomprehensible horsey jargon in his support.

John Grey looked serious, testing the ground with his heel.

Nick slipped Chieftain's Son into the stalls first. Mo followed on Fourcade, one of Brant's horses.

Mike signalled to Joe. Joe dropped his arm. Danny threw the lever.

Both horses sprang out together. They were upsides to the first marker.

Fourcade gained a head, then a length. Daylight appeared at the second. The grey was four lengths adrift at the third.

The gap widened all the way to the finish.

John Grey rubbed his neck with an enormous red handkerchief.

James Brant walked over to the Land-Rover Discovery

he had bought and sat in the front passenger seat, waiting to be driven. Fourcade was worth keeping, he decided.

Tom Fisher had to sit in the back.

Jackie Pilgrim jumped into the driving seat of the Mercedes, eager for confirmation.

'Didn't I say?'

'Move,' his father said, lighting another cigarette.

Jackie started the car. They bumped slowly along the Ridgeway track.

'Well?'

'It could still win,' John Pilgrim said, staring out of the side window, 'Slow horses pull carts.'

'You've seen it with your own eyes.'

'Beaten in a photo. It wasn't hanging about then.'

'Which is why,' said Jackie.

'Why?'

'It'll start favourite. Jolly.'

'Might. It's not a science.'

'We lay it at slightly better odds than anyone else. Punters'll come up out of the ground. Happened before.'

'*If* it loses.'

John Pilgrim detested the idea.

'Guaranteed. Pay the tax-man. Pay everyone . . .' said Jackie, temptingly.

'Always have – "Pilgrim Always Pays".'

He was determined to have nothing to do with it.

They reached the smoother road and picked up speed.

'It's our big chance to get straight,' Jackie went on, confidently. 'Think about Mum.'

John Pilgrim thought about Brenda. She imagined that they were rich, because they lived in a four-bedroomed house and she had a Mini of her own. She left figures to him, they were his job. He thought about the fat woman from the Inland Revenue who had served his summons and the small fortune he owed in Capital Gains, according to them, when he had lost everything. If he could sell his pitches on the racecourses, he would, but that was not allowed. He could only pass them on to his son. But his son did not want them.

He did not want to worry Brenda. He wondered if . . .

He opened the side window and flicked his cigarette out.

'I must give these damn things up . . .' he said.

Nick jumped down from Chieftain's Son in the yard. Mike lifted off the saddle.

'Going backwards,' Nick complained. 'Slow as a church. Beaten a bus ride . . .'

He led the grey towards his box, disconsolately.

Mike carried the saddle to the tack-room, followed by Frances.

'Mike . . .'

She was suddenly suspicious.

'What?'

He carried on walking. She ran after him.

'What've you got under there?'

'Hmm?'

'If it's what I think, Mike, I don't agree . . .'

He went into the tack-room and tossed the weight-cloth aside.

At Newbury, Mike gave Ronnie Foulkes his instructions, before he mounted Chieftain's Son.

'Let him run his own race. Stay within the rules. Don't pick your bat up too much — hands and heels. You're drawn Three, which is fine.'

*

In the hurly-burly of the betting ring, John Pilgrim's 'joint' stood in the middle of the middle rank. On-course bookmakers wait for dead men's shoes and move up by seniority. Old men hold the prime positions.

Nine runners were listed alphabetically.

Chieftain's Son was evens-favourite on all the boards.

Jackie Pilgrim rubbed the chalked price out. He replaced it with five to four.

Punters moved forward.

Their tic-tac took bets from the 'Firms' on the rails in rapid sign language, calling to John Pilgrim 'You've laid five thousand to four thousand to Gorman.'

'Five hundred to four hundred, Chieftain's Son,' said a voice.

'Five hundred to four hundred, ticket number 214,' said Pilgrim.

Jackie Pilgrim wrote figures in his Field Book feverishly as they were called out.

'Ten thousand to eight thousand, Chieftain's Son,' John Grey said, offering crisp fifty pound notes.

Pilgrim paused and looked hard at John Grey. He was a known 'face' and it made him uncomfortable.

He took the money and put it in the bag, without checking it.

'Ten thousand to eight thousand, Mr Grey.'

No ticket was given, an honour to the professional.

The bag attached to the jointed tripod – the 'joint' – filled with cash as punters pressed forward, just as Jackie had predicted.

'Ten hundred to eight hundred, Chieftain's Son.'

'Ten hundred to eight hundred, ticket number 215.'

'Forty pounds, Chieftain's Son.'

'Fifty pounds to forty, ticket number 216.'

'You've laid twelve and half thousand to ten thousand to Fryers,' said the tic-tac, taking another bet from the rails . . .

Jockeys were mounted. One by one, the nine runners were led to the course. Nick and Mo struggled to hold the grey and stop him taking a line of his own, but he burst free at the gate and followed the others, cantering past the crowded stands on the way to the start. The commentator described them on the PA system.

'Next number three, Chieftain's Son, the clear favourite for this six-furlong race, a handsome grey ridden by Ronnie Foulkes.'

Mike handed Nick a small roll of bank notes, held by an elastic band.

'Here. Put this on.'

Nick stared at him, surprised.

'With Pilgrim. Be quick.'

He walked on to join Frances and Tom Fisher, on their way to the stands, without looking back.

Mo grabbed his arm. They ran towards Tattersalls.

The Judge studied his colours and set his wire sight-line. The Starter called out the numbers. The handlers checked the girths and led the horses into the stalls, odd numbers first. Chieftain's Son refused and was blindfolded.

A crowd of punters surrounded John Pilgrim's joint. Cash was being handed over in small and large bets, in coins and bank notes. The tic-tac signalled frantically, as bets came in from the rails.

Jackie Pilgrim grinned as the bag filled.

'Five hundred to four hundred, Chieftain's Son.'

'Five hundred to four hundred, ticket number 287.'

'Five pounds to four pounds, Chieftain's Son.'

John Pilgrim tossed five one-pound coins into the bag.

'Five pounds to four pounds, ticket number 288.'

Nick was next in line. He handed over the roll of notes.

'Five hundred to four hundred, Chieftain's Son, Mr Pilgrim.'

Pilgrim paused, took off the elastic band, counted the notes and looked at Jackie, meaningfully. Then he said, slowly.

'Five hundred to four hundred, ticket number 289 . . .'

Chieftain's Son was last in the stalls.

'They're under Starter's Orders . . .' the commentator said.

The gates snapped open and the horses burst out in an explosion of colour.

'. . . And they're off!'

The bookmakers shut up shop and turned round to watch the race.

Jackie Pilgrim hurriedly calculated, adding columns in his Field Book. His father checked the bag.

'How much?'

Jackie smiled, proudly.

'Fifty-five thousand. Near enough.'

His father almost smiled.

'Say it again.

'Half of it cash. Fifty-five thousand . . .'

They did not watch the race. They could hardly bear to

98

hear the commentary. Chieftain's Son was well placed behind the leaders, Rose Felicia making the running.

He moved up into second place and the commentator raised his pitch hysterically.

'. . . In the final furlong and it's Chieftain's Son making a challenge on the inside of Rose Felicia, these two now, Chieftain's Son neck and neck with Rose Felicia as they race to the line . . .

The Judge sighted them with his wire, then turned to the Official Announcer.

'Photograph,' he said.

'The result is a photograph for first place between horse Number Three and horse Number Seven . . .' the Official Announcer relayed to the public.

The Racecourse Technical Services' technicians began work at once, developing. The crowds waited anxiously.

John Pilgrim lit a cigarette and turned to stare at his son . . .

Frances was delighted.

'He won! He won!'

'Might just,' Mike said laconically, as they walked to the Winner's Enclosure.

'I didn't bet!' Tom Fisher shouted furiously from behind.

'Why not? I did.'

'At the trial – it was going bloody backwards.'

'I told you – training and racing . . .'

Tom Fisher caught up with them.

'You fixed it!'

Mike's face gave nothing away.

'Smile,' he said. 'You've won a cup.'

Tom Fisher glared.

'That's it. I'm definitely taking my horse away.'

The Judge scrutinized the monitor screen showing the leading horses frozen on the line. Chieftain's Son had his nose in front.

'First, Number Three. Second, Number Seven. Third, Number Five,' he said to the Official Announcer.

The awful words reverberated.

'. . . in racecard order, first Number Three, Chieftain's Son . . .'

John Pilgrim was aghast. Jackie wished the ground would open up.

They could not believe it. The world had ended. The universe had ended.

The first punter offered his winning ticket before the announcement was over.

It was Nick, with Mo beside him.

Pilgrim looked at the ticket, automatically.

'Number 289,' he said to Jackie, in a small voice.

Jackie ran his finger down the column.

'Wins five hundred to four hundred. Nine hundred.'

Nine ten-pound notes, wrapped crosswise by a tenth, made an easily recognisable one-hundred-pound bundle. He counted out nine of these. Nick stopped him.

'Give me one hundred and fifty and we're straight.'

It did not seem to sink in.

'Right? Mr Pilgrim?'

'Right,' said Pilgrim, after a pause. 'We're straight.'

He split a bundle and handed Nick the money.

'I'm a witness,' said Mo.

They stood aside for the next punter in line. He did not have a ticket.

'What do we have down for Mr Grey?' Pilgrim said, painfully.

Jackie consulted the book.

'Ten thousand to eight thousand – eighteen thousand pounds.'

Pilgrim stared impassively ahead. Jackie waited for instructions. John Grey smiled, faintly. There was a brief pause.

'Well, come on, pay the man.'

Jackie dug in the bag, making a hole in the cash.

' "Pilgrim Always Pays" – that was my father's motto.'

'Thank you,' John Grey said. He pocketed the large wad of notes without checking them and strolled away.

Chieftain's Son wore the Arkenfield rug and stood for a few minutes in the position of glory: the number one stall in the Winner's Enclosure. Tom Fisher had his photograph taken, trying to smile.

An official made a short speech.

'On behalf of Dalefords Estate, I present the challenge cup to the winning owner, Mr Tom Fisher. Congratulations. Trainer, Mr Michael Hardy, receives a signed print . . .'

A ripple of claps, cheers from the Arkenfield connections, and Tom Fisher looked at his small cup.

'Horses away!' Another official dismissed.

Tom Fisher felt like a fool. He had not had a pound on his own winner.

'Think of the prize money,' Mike said, as Tom Fisher stalked off to join his friends, 'I'll deduct my training fees from that . . .'

*

The last race of the meeting was under way. Wise racegoers were making for the car-parks, to get out before the rush.

Sandwich-board evangelists raised their messages.

One black notice held high read: 'BE SURE YOUR SIN WILL FIND YOU OUT'.

The open-mouthed bag hanging on the joint was nearly empty.

'Ticket Number 288,' John Pilgrim said.

Jackie looked in the Field Book.

'Five pounds to four pounds, nine pounds.'

Pilgrim counted nine one-pound coins into the hand held out in front of him.

'Ta,' said the punter, moving away. Another took his place, proffering a ticket. There were dozens more behind.

'Ticket Number 216,' he said in a hollow voice.

'Fifty pounds to forty, ninety pounds . . .'

Jackie reached into the bag, took out one of the few bundles of notes left and split it.

Pilgrim took the money and handed it over.

'Ticket Number 215.'

Jackie read out, 'Ten hundred to eight hundred, eighteen hundred.'

He looked up at his father.

'Pay the man, Jackie.'

Jackie tried to catch his father's eye. There wasn't enough money to pay.

'Dad – we've run out,' he said in a low whisper.

Pilgrim brought out a few more bundles of notes from his inside pockets. He tossed them into the bag.

'Ticket Number 214,' he said, taking another punter's winning ticket.

'Dad – there isn't enough . . .'

Pilgrim brought loose coins out of his trouser pocket and flung them into the bag.

'Hurry up. Ticket Number 267.'

'Dad –'

The tic-tac felt in his pockets and threw in eighteen pounds. Jackie found a ten-pound note and a few coins.

John Pilgrim held his head up and looked at the punters. There seemed to be even more of them.

How many were there? Fifty? A hundred?

'Pay the man,' he said, his face contorting. 'Pilgrim always pays.'

Jackie cringed behind the tripod. The tic-tac got down from the wooden stool, preparing to run.

John Pilgrim stared defiantly ahead.

'Pay the man. Pay the man,' he repeated . . .

FIVE

Spring faded. Hopes for the new crop of two-year-olds were tempered by results. Wonder horses racing in the early trials of the season were beaten by ordinary horses. Ten-thousand-guinea rags romped home ahead of hundred-thousand-guinea favourites. Accidents happened. Legs broke; tendons strained; diseases attacked.

Everyone said, 'That's racing!'

Arkenfield survived the flu virus. The 'Equaid' story was eclipsed in the racing press by new scandals. Complaining owners moved on, complaining to new trainers. Horses were sold to buy better horses. They were often worse. Winners were no easier to find, and losers were everywhere, eating hay.

James Brant bulldozed his way forward.

Blacksmith's Boy – a colt with no chance of winning – won at Newbury by half a length. Brant was unprepared. No guests were invited. If Kath had not been with him, only the yard staff would have witnessed him receiving a crystal bowl.

He decided to buy a very expensive yearling. Perhaps big money was the answer to success. At Newmarket, he paid a ridiculous sum for a well-bred colt, which turned out to be lame. If Mike had not found it to be a windsucker as well, and Stewart Staunton had not been able to verify it, he would have lost every guinea he bid. Horses were not commodities to be returned, like cars, if something was wrong.

The best brains in racing made mistakes. Sound business principles, learned over the years, were of little use in finding a good horse – one good enough to win a Classic.

Mike bought a horse called Welfare State from Hugo Latimer, which Frances had recommended as a bargain.

Joe Hogan disagreed.

'Latimer's not stupid,' he said, as they watched Danny ride the colt on the gallops.

'Meaning we are . . .?' Frances asked, defensively.

Mike pointed out Welfare State's virtues of action and conformation.

'Then why did Hugo sell him – to you of all people?'

There was no point in trying to conceal anything from Joe.

'He's got a temperament problem,' Mike said.

Oh, well that sounds promising,' Joe laughed mockingly.

'Haven't you got any faith in your Guv'nor, Joe?' Frances wanted to know.

'You might get him going. But who's going to pay thirty-five grand?'

'He does think we're stupid.'

Frances and Mike exchanged a knowing smile.

Danny trotted up on Welfare State to receive more instructions, followed by Mo and Nick, who were keeping apart from the new horse.

'Six furlongs up, then back. Easy canter. That doesn't meant gallop, Danny. He's new, so let him settle. Right. Go.'

They watched the horses disappear over the top of the gallops.

Joe was insistent.

'You were going to tell me about the new owner.'

Mike pointed to the old blue Alvis in the distance, bumping its way slowly towards them along the edge of the all-weather track.

'John Grey?'

James Brant sat at his desk in his shirtsleeves, eating toast and marmalade. He had shaved and brushed his hair and was reading the racing page of the *Daily Gazette* with intensity. It was one of his five morning papers.

Kath was still in her dressing gown and slippers. She had less energy than him, first thing in the morning. Her hair fell over her eyes as she poured him a mug of tea.

'Ah, yes, here, listen,' Brant said, reading a paragraph out loud, ' "Brant said . . . 'I spotted Mike's promise and talent immediately and persuaded him to join me in this exciting venture . . .' " '

Kath poured a cup of tea for herself and yawned.

He went on.

'Blah . . . blah . . . this is me again at the end: "We may not have Classic horses yet, but it won't be long. When we do, watch out for us," he said." ' Brant was delighted. 'Well, what do you think?'

'It must've been a slow day,' Kath yawned again.

Brant picked up the telephone and rang the *Gazette* at once.

'Sports. Billy Dawson, please . . .'

John Grey looked rueful and apologetic.

'No cash,' he said, simply.

'You what!'

Mike and Frances were horrified. Joe Hogan stared

resignedly at the horses cantering by. He could have guessed as much.

'A dog in Trap 2 ran wide.'

Mike was unsure whether he was joking or not.

'He means it,' said Frances, after a pause.

'Afraid I do,' John Grey added, 'Not that sort of cash.'

Mike strode off to his Land-Rover in disgust, without saying a word.

'I didn't promise to buy him . . .' John Grey said, lamely.

'I hope Mike agrees,' Frances warned, hiding her concern.

Joe found nothing useful to add and wandered over to the Land-Rover where Mike was sitting in the driving seat, tapping the steering wheel and staring at the horizon, waiting for the horses to return. Joe was about to say something, when Mike snapped,

'Don't crow!'

'Wasn't going to,' Joe said, quickly: 'Not in my nature. Plan B, then?'

Mike turned his head.

'B . . .?'

'For Brant. Got to be worth a try . . .'

Mike thought for a second, then picked up the mobile telephone.

Kath cleared the breakfast dishes off her husband's desk. She was used to him working as soon as he was awake and closed her mind to it. It was why he had his breakfast in the study. There were regular telephone calls before eight o'clock.

She was vaguely aware that he was talking to Mike.

'No, I'm not interested in other people's rejects.'

She tried to remove his half-empty mug of tea.

'I haven't finished with that,' he said, grabbing the mug from her and going on in the same commanding voice she hated to hear so early. 'Your job is to concentrate on Black Deed and have him ready for Saturday. You're fussing again, Mike. There's nothing wrong with him. His blood-count's fine. I'm not going to argue. He will run.'

He slammed down the telephone and glared at his wife.

She looked at him steadily. He was the same every morning.

Mike did not speak after listening to James Brant. Joe climbed into the passenger seat next to him and shrugged. They waited in silence for the string to return.

Frances got into the Alvis and talked to John Grey intently as they bumped their way back to the yard.

There were no horses in sight.

Mike glanced at his watch after five minutes.

Suddenly, a horse appeared on the skyline. It had no rider. They recognized it as the new colt, Welfare State. They dived out of the Land-Rover and ran to intercept, but the horse galloped past them, wide-eyed and beyond control.

Rosie the Dragon was quite taken with the young man who appeared in the office later that morning. He was good-looking, for one thing. He wore casual, trendy clothes unlike anything worn in the village and spoke in a well-educated voice. He reminded her of someone on television.

'I'm Billy Dawson,' he smiled, 'I'm a journalist.'

She made him a cup of tea and while Mike was busy, asked him about all the famous people he knew.

*

Welfare State had reached the yard ahead of them. He was eating grass by the hedge outside when they found him. He was undamaged. When Danny returned, limping dramatically, half an hour later, his explanation was simply, 'He threw a wobbly, Guv.'

Billy Dawson waited an hour. Mike refused to see him, remembering with distaste the stories the tabloid had printed during the 'Equaid' hearing. He learned then that 'no comment' was the only response to make to people who could twist words better than Sally.

But John Grey spoke to Dawson at great length.

'The plan is,' he said afterwards, '*The Daily Gazette* will buy Welfare State for thirty-eight thousand five hundred. You will get thirty-five thousand and train him. I will get three thousand five hundred.'

'What for?'

'Commission. Only fair, don't you think?'

'No – I meant why does a newspaper want to buy a horse?'

'Profile. They run a readership competition: "Own a racehorse for a year." Publicity. Sort of equine bingo . . .'

Two hours after Mike had reluctantly agreed, the power of the press showed itself again in an odd telephone call.

Rosie was thrilled.

'It's Pattie Roman – for you!'

'Who?'

'You know – the singer,' said Rosie, who watched television constantly in her free time.

'Never heard of her,' said Mike, who hardly ever did.

'She's brilliant! She says she wants to come and look round the yard. She read the bit in the paper.'

She arrived in a red Ferrari F40 four days later, in time to see First Lot pulling out. The lads gathered round to see her. Mo wore a fan's T-shirt under her padded waistcoat. John Grey dressed in an elegant tweed suit from Gieves and Hawkes, ten years old at least. James Brant smelled of aftershave. Kath had made an effort, even though it was too early for her, and Frances was trim in hacking jacket and jodhpurs.

Mike looked as if he had just finished mucking-out.

A young man leapt out of the driving seat. He wore a pale wide-shouldered suit, with pale handmade shoes. He skipped round to open the passenger door.

They all heard her voice, before they could see her through the smoked glass.

'It's OK, Pete. I can manage a door.'

Pattie Roman raised herself out of the low car. She was dressed in jeans, with a waxed sleeveless jacket over a warm top and flat 'sensible' shoes. She was very beautiful. She was black.

Mike stepped forward to shake her hand.

'Hallo, I'm Mike Hardy.'

'Hallo, Mike Hardy,' she said, softly, 'I'm Pattie. This is my manager, Pete.'

She enjoyed her morning enormously. She watched First Lot standing by Mike's Land-Rover, halfway up the gallops. James Brant pointed out every horse in his string, as they cantered past in pairs.

'That's Blacksmith's Boy, a winner, with Dangerous Lady. We've got great hopes for those two.'

He was bright-eyed and full of enthusiasm.

'And that's Black Deed on this side. He runs on Saturday.'

'Maybe,' said Mike, curtly.

'The vet can't find anything—'

'He's not right.' Mike emphasized, strongly.

Brant overruled him, showing Pattie his authority.

'Nevertheless – I say he runs.'

She turned to Mike.

'What's wrong with him?'

Mike said nothing in front of Brant, but she persisted.

'Instinct?'

'You know horses?'

'A bit . . . Now I like that!' she called out. The next pair were cantering down. Danny rode Welfare State on the nearside.

'He's not mine,' Brant said in a flat voice, looking the other way, as if there wasn't a horse in sight.

'Is he for sale? she asked Mike, sweetly.

'You're just too late. I didn't think you were serious . . .'

She stood uncomfortably close to him.

James Brant left before the work-riding was over. Kath was glad to get out of the cold wind. Frances went with them.

The string returned, blowing slightly, and circled, jigging with excitement. Welfare State objected to joining the others. He started to buck, twisting his body and laying his ears flat against his neck. Danny tried to stay on. Raucous shouts of encouragement filled the air, but he was soon tossed to the ground. He lay there, pounding the turf with his fists in frustration and anger. The lads laughed.

Welfare State ran off a little way and stopped. He shook his head and began grazing, unconcernedly.

'Everyone stay still. Don't move.'

Mike stalked quietly towards him.

Pattie Roman walked slowly to a position where she could stop Welfare State running back on to the gallops.

Without taking his eyes off the horse, Mike said, urgently,

'Get back in the Land-Rover. You might get hurt.'

'I know what I'm doing,' she replied, taking no notice.

Mike's voice was quiet, but firm.

'Pattie, please. Do as I say.'

He edged closer. Just when he was almost in reach of the reins, Welfare State trotted off a few more yards and resumed cropping grass. Mike tried again.

'Head him towards me,' Pattie called.

Mike approached from a different angle.

Again, he moved at the last second. This time, Pattie blocked his way. He stopped, nearly within touching distance.

Then Pattie turned on her heel and walked away. She put a hand in her pocket and rustled a piece of paper.

The horse pricked up his ears and followed her.

She continued walking and rustling the paper until Welfare State nudged her in the back. Then she turned and caught him.

'They always fall for it,' she laughed.

The Daily Gazette's rival newspaper was *The Argos*. Both competed in scandals about television stars and sports personalities. The public good was served by destroying the careers of politicians like Charles Burton. They had opposing views on everything. But topless models, competitions, and excellent football and racing coverage gave each a large circulation, which they constantly sought to increase at the other's expense.

They were equally unscrupulous.

The Gazette's 'Own a Racehorse' competition was a big success. Minds on *The Argos* worked hard to find a way to counter it.

They pored over files of earlier stories and splashed with:

From Bix – the Man Who Knows.
Trainer Mike Hardy – remember him of the Equaid Doping Affair? – seems to have a curious KNACK of getting out of trouble a little TOO easily.
Soon to be divorced Hardy, DARLING of *The Daily Gazette*, was recently fined for DOPING one of his horses.
How did MILLIONAIRE-OWNER James Brant and Hardy – who are not the BEST of friends – think they would escape punishment?
Come on boys, play the rules!

A photograph of Mike, looking furtive, headed the piece. It had been taken after the Jockey Club hearing, when he was trying to escape from the photographers.

'Who is this Bix character?' Mike wanted to know.

'Doesn't exist,' Billy Dawson said. 'He's their little creation. They have a saying – "If it's too hot for you – the byline is Bix". The entire editorial staff contribute. I'd say this came from Adam Forsythe. He passes for what they call their Racing Correspondent.'

'Libel?'

'Got fifty grand to spare? Leave it. You can't stop them.'

'If it's going to turn nasty, we'll forget the whole thing.'

Billy Dawson was emphatic.

'You try to pull out now – the *Gazette*'ll have you up to your armpits in lawyers.'

A moment later, seeing Mike's face, he relented.

'Look, maybe there's something I can do . . .'

They continued to discuss arrangements for what Billy called a 'Photo Opportunity' – a series of glamour pictures to enliven the competition and keep it rolling. Mike hated the idea.

'It'll look great,' Billy said, 'if we could get someone like Pattie Roman, as well as the girls. Do you a lot of good. Friend of the rich and famous and all that. Trainer to the stars . . .'

Mike's nose wrinkled in disgust.

'I'd rather have Mouse Sampson . . .'

'Fine, whoever,' said Billy, confidently. 'Who's Mouse Sampson?'

'I thought you were a Racing Correspondent, too? She's a lady jockey – one of the best in the country.'

'Oh, Don Sampson's wife. Isn't she called Cathy?'

Mike had a simple theory about Welfare State: he did not like men. He had thought about it since watching the way the horse reacted to Pattie Roman. It was unusual in an expensive thoroughbred, because they were so carefully treated in training yards, but too common in other breeds. Some men still believed in giving a horse a good thrashing to make them obedient. They were even proud of it.

He had tested the theory with Mo riding him. There was no repeat of the bucking behaviour he had shown with Danny. But he would not risk an inexperienced apprentice like her in an important race.

Cathy 'Mouse' Sampson agreed to ride 'work' on Welfare

114

State and give her opinion. She turned up early, before First Lot pulled out, driving a new BMW. A small perky blonde, dressed in waxed sleeveless jacket, jodhpurs and boots.

'Morning, Mike!'

'You must be doing well,' Mike said, looking at the car.

'You're joking. Five rides in three weeks? The car's Don's. Being married to a champion has some compensations.'

Mike showed her the horse.

'What's wrong with him?' she asked.

Mike looked at her, innocently.

'Mike – I've been around trainers long enough – a woman only gets a ride if there's a dodge – or if the trainer fancies her. Which is it?'

'Both,' Mike laughed. 'No, no dodge. He just hates men.'

Mouse patted Welfare State on the side of his neck.

'I know how you feel, old chap. Right. Let's do it.'

Mike legged her into the saddle and he and Joe followed First Lot up to the gallops in the Land-Rover.

Mo watched Mouse ride, her face filled with admiration. Mouse was everything Mo wanted to be. She was pretty and successful, a brilliant jockey who could get the best out of any horse. Nick rode with her, on Black Deed, to set a control.

Eventually, Mouse trotted back to where Mike was standing.

'Well?'

'Don't you dare put anyone else on him, Mike Hardy.' She slipped off lightly and handed the reins to Joe.

'That good?'

'Best I've sat on, bar none. When's his first run?'

'Newbury, Saturday. Can you do it?'

'Mike, I'd love to.'

'You're on. Let's get some breakfast. Joe, hack them home. Give 'em a pick of grass somewhere. Get this one dressed over, ready.'

The *Gazette* girls arrived in a minibus at nine o'clock, exactly as arranged. Billy Dawson introduced them to Mike and Mouse Sampson.

'Meet Mandy 'n' Sandy.'

They were both stunningly beautiful and almost identical. Their make-up was perfect, their smiles matched.

A middle-aged woman carrying a large cardboard case and a rough-looking, unshaven young man with a pigtail, got out of the minibus with them.

'This is Lionel, our star photographer. This is Betty, our star make-up artist.'

While they rigged up lights and reflector boards, others turned up to see the action. Frances drove in five minutes later in her Rover. Mo and the lads peered from boxes. In one of them Welfare State was being washed down and groomed.

Pattie Roman's Ferrari snarled to a standstill at half past nine and she got out, looking every inch a star, in a white silk suit.

She kissed Mike on the cheek, called him 'darling' and prepared herself for the photographic session. Frances, feeling frumpy in her hacking jacket, detected an easy sexual chemistry between Mike and the black singer which made her uncomfortable. She did not believe the talk about Pattie Roman wanting to buy a horse.

'Do I have to wear all this stuff?' Mouse wanted to know, as Betty applied powder to her face in dainty puffs.

'We just have to tone you down a little bit,' said Betty.

Lionel brought two new racing saddles from the minibus. Mike was appalled at the profligacy.

'Places, everyone,' Lionel said, 'I'd like Pattie on this side and er . . . Mouse on the other and Sandy 'n' Mandy beside them . . .'

He angled his fingers and composed a tableau round a gap to be filled by Welfare State.

When he was satisfied, the horse was led out to stand in the centre.

'Right. Ready. Could you each hold one of the thingys?'

He meant the reins.

'Girls, let's be having you . . .'

Sandy and Mandy stripped to matching red two-piece swimsuits and smiled. The lads cheered.

James Brant stopped his car near the entrance. He walked slowly into the yard, looking at the scene in astonishment. He was still angry about what he had read.

'What's this . . .?'

Mike went quickly to meet him, feeling embarrassed.

'They'll be done shortly. Billy said we should counter the *Argos* story with positive publicity . . .'

Pattie Roman waved at him, cheerily.

'Nice to see you again, Pattie,' he smiled, ignoring Mike. He strolled into the middle of the carefully arranged shot and said to Billy,

'What say you to a few snaps of me? As patron and senior owner? Welcoming Pattie – and Mouse – and these young ladies – to the yard?'

'Great idea,' Billy said, hiding his scorn.

'I think I should hold the horse, don't you?'

*

Mike was still worried about Black Deed. What was the matter with him? He felt sure the animal was not fit to run. He had learned to trust some of his feelings, but he could not always express them in words. Stewart Staunton had given the all-clear. Brant had insisted, quite reasonably, that in the absence of medical evidence of unsoundness, the horse would run as entered and declared.

The Daily Gazette ran the colour picture two days later. It was not as cheap as Mike had feared. Welfare State dominated the frame magnificently, under the heading 'Your Horse's Top Form'. Fun-loving enthusiasm for racing shone in the eyes of the models. Mouse Sampson and Pattie Roman smiled appreciatively at James Brant.

Bix in *The Argos* the same day had:

> 'It seems that MACHO Mike Hardy, he of the DOPING scandal, sets more than horses racing . . . Female pulses quicken at the sight of him. Since the bust-up with WIFE Sally, Hardy has been seeing rather a lot of PRETTY neighbour Frances Ross, daughter of INJURED Jack Ross. He is obviously not a man of SINGULAR tastes either. Recently he has been seen in the company of blonde and bubbly jock-ette, Cathy 'Mouse' Sampson, wife of CHAMPION Don, as well as FUN-LOVING black singer Pattie Roman . . .'

Readers who saw both papers drew their conclusions, sniggered with envy and placed their bets on Welfare State.

Billy Dawson defended himself against Mike's fury.

'It didn't come from me! I had a word with Adam Forsythe. I told him to lay off.'

'It must've come from you. Who else?'

'Someone here in the yard. We were in the same House.'

Adam Forsythe had attended the same public school as Billy Dawson who seemed to think that this meant something.

Mike dismissed it all.

'You're both bloody journalists, whatever your motto.'

The column offended Frances the most. She said it could ruin her career, by association. Her father laughed.

But he did not mention the singer.

The two horses were ready to be boxed for racing. Mike had spent an hour with Black Deed. He was still convinced that something was wrong. He had walked him round. He had felt his legs. He had studied his eyes. He had held his ears. He had looked at his facial expression.

He had known the horse as a yearling, fresh from the Sales.

There were many things he could not account for. He often knew, in the middle of the night, when a horse was sick. He spoke to them in a language that had nothing to do with words, and they spoke to him.

'It's his attitude . . .' he tried to say.

Brant would have none of it:

'He's bone idle. Black Deed runs on Saturday. That's an end to it.'

Pattie Roman arrived in the office when Mike was trying to explain to Frances that her career was not at risk.

'Aha!' Pattie cried, melodramatically, 'my lover and my rival. Caught in the act!'

Frances was shocked at first. Pattie was ebullient. Her laugh was infectious.

'If I had a horse for every time I've been linked with a bloke . . . Look, they're grubby people. Stay above it. Let's go racing. We'll present a united, unbothered front. Come on, hup, two, three . . .'

Gazette girls were at the racecourse. There were twelve of them scantily dressed in red. The Sports Editor wore a brown trilby and a tweed suit. Welfare State was bedecked in a magnificent red rug with *The Gazette* discreetly cornered, within the advertising rules. Copies of *The Gazette* were given away, along with red emblazoned plastic bags. Red hoardings along the track advertised *The Gazette*, 'The Winner'.

James Brant had words in private with Paul Steele, a wizened, wasted, middle-aged jockey who needed a winner.

He was riding Black Deed in the second.

Billy Dawson wanted Mike to meet the Sports Editor, David Fox.

'Later. In the stands, before the off.'

Mike concentrated on Black Deed, his first runner of the meeting. He stripped off the paddock-sheet and legged Steele into the plate.

Walking alongside, as Danny led the horse, he gave his instructions to the jockey.

'Have him handy until the two. Then let him run. If he fades, don't be hard on him. And don't hit him. Hands and heels.'

Steele nodded, but seemed unhappy.

Kath solved the problem of where the *Argos* story came from.

She accused her husband, 'It was you. You told *The Argos* Mike was having affairs.'

'No.'

'Didn't you think what it might do to Arkenfield?'

'It was a mistake. A man rang. Adam Forsythe. Said he was from *The Gazette*. Wanted background . . .'

'And you just gave it to him?'

'How was I supposed to know?'

Kath left him by the parade ring.

'Where are you going?'

'To watch the race with Mike,' she said, without looking back.

Billy Dawson introduced his boss.

'Mike – this is David Fox, my editor. He's come to see what our readers get for their money.'

Fox was a small man, with friendly eyes.

'We're doing our best to raise the image of British racing,' he said, sounding sincere, 'unlike a rival we won't mention. *The Gazette* doesn't need scandal . . .'

The eyes took in Pattie Roman and Frances, but remained friendly.

Mike shook his hand, respectfully.

'Excuse me, Mr Fox. I have a runner in this.'

They all turned to watch the race.

'And they're off!' the commentator said, starting his litany.

Kath excused her way up the steps of the Owners' and Trainers' stand. She found Mike, with Frances and Pattie Roman on either side of him, and made room for herself between them and the editor.

James Brant followed her, pushing and shouting angrily.

David Fox could hardly see over him when he took his place.

Black Deed was lying third.

All binoculars were trained on the course. The distant horses appeared on the bend.

'Black Deed is making a challenge . . .'

Paul Steele lifted his bat at the two-furlong pole. He needed the money Brant had offered. He wanted to win. Black Deed responded well, surging nicely into second place. Steele had taken money throughout his career to stop horses, but it was unusual to get conflicting instructions from the owner. He suspected a job. When he felt Black Deed labouring slightly, he lifted his bat again. He would rather win for money than lose for money. He was almost upsides with the leader, on the rail. Nearly neck and neck . . .

'Use your bloody whip, man!' Brant roared from the stands.

'No! I told him not to! What the hell does he think he's doing?'

Mike was furious. He could not understand why Steele was blatantly disobeying his instructions.

The editor counted the lashes in disgust.

'That's more than the permitted ten already,' he said.

Amid the roar of the crowds, there were boos of revulsion as the two leaders thundered towards the finish, with Black Deed struggling to hold his head in front and Steele lashing him hard on the quarters.

'Atta boy!' Brant leapt up and down, knocking Fox's elbow in his uncontrolled zeal.

Black Deed crossed the line a neck in front.

Mike looked suddenly concerned. He pushed his way

past Brant, who was shouting in triumph, and ran down the steps towards the edge of the course.

Joe and Danny reached Black Deed first. The colt was distressed, heaving and covered in sweat. Blood streamed from his nostrils. Red cuts flared on his quarters.

Paul Steele remained in the saddle, staring straight ahead, impassively, as Danny led him in.

Mixed reactions came from the crowds. Some cheered Steele as an old-time hard master, while others booed his appallingly cruel display.

Mike arrived to find Joe cursing.

'He's broken a blood vessel, Guv.'

Mike stood outside the Weighing Room, waiting for Paul Steele to come out. Stewards were looking at the weals on Black Deed and calling for the vet. Joe and Danny tried to soothe the horse as it hung its head in the Winner's Enclosure.

Brant was there to receive his prize – another crystal bowl – from a subdued presenter. Kath was not with him. There were few claps from the small group gathered round. Serious-looking officials came in and out of the Weighing Room, conferring in low voices.

Paul Steele appeared in Brant's colours, spattered with mud, his mind alive with events and the effort he had made to produce a winner.

'The horse may never race again,' said Mike, viciously. 'You'll be lucky if *you* can, you bastard, when I've finished with you.'

Steele avoided Mike's eyes and said nothing. He was looking at James Brant, holding the bowl and talking to a man from the press while another took his photograph.

'What did he offer you? Holiday in Tenerife? What?'

The jockey stared uncomfortably down at his mud-flecked boots.

'Rules 15 and 153. You'll be suspended for improper use, for starters. So I hope it was worth it.'

The *Gazette* girls trooped festively through the Members' Enclosure on their way to the Parade Ring.

James Brant had left early. He had no interest in the rest of the card. Kath had stayed on, to see Mike's next runner, Welfare State. She had not seen Mike who had been busy in the racecourse stables with the vet, looking at Black Deed. She tagged along with Frances and Pattie Roman and lost five pounds on the Tote. Pattie bought them each an ice-cream and they tried to forget Black Deed's race.

John Grey had not backed Black Deed. Mike had said the horse was not right. He risked a hundred pounds on Welfare State, but was not in a betting mood. He was not the only one who abhorred the sight of blood. The disgraceful spectacle of Black Deed being whipped tainted the rest of the meeting for some of the tender-hearted, while others said,

'That's racing!'

Mike hurried from the stables and ran into the man from the press he had seen talking to James Brant earlier. A fair-haired, scruffy-looking young man in a sports jacket. Before he had said a word, the photographer with him whirred his automatic camera and took several shots.

'Can we have your reaction, Mike?'

'Who are you?'

'Adam Forsythe of *The Argos*.'

Mike studied his face for a moment.

'Yes, you can. No comment.'

He pushed past him and continued walking. Adam Forsythe and the photographer ran after him.

'Can we ask if it's true that Welfare State has changed trainer?'

'What?'

'We understand that as of now, he's returned to Hugo Latimer.'

Mike paused. He was shocked, then suspicious.

'You're joking,' he said.

'Do you want to comment?'

'No. I've nothing to say.'

'Is it true, though?' Adam Forsythe persisted.

Mike hurried on towards the Parade Ring.

'Like I said. I've got nothing to say.'

The runners delicately paced around. On the private green lawn in the centre, the connections of each horse gathered in groups. Throngs of punters outside the ring pressed against the rails. They craned and peered to see the horses parading by. They checked the numbers against their race-cards. They studied the size and conformation and well-being of each animal. Some paid more attention to the size and conformation of the connections in the belief that more meant more chance of winning. They each made their choice of likely winner.

Mike saw Hugo Latimer standing with David Fox of the *Daily Gazette*, in the middle of the ring, surrounded by glamorous red *Gazette* girls. David Ware was there with his arm round one of them. Mouse Sampson stood next to him, looking small and trim in the garish red colours of the newspaper. Billy Dawson was making her laugh.

'What the hell's going on?' Mike demanded to know.

Billy Dawson detached himself from Mouse and strolled up to where Mike was standing by himself.

'I'm sorry, Mike . . .'

David Fox came over and said, sincerely,

'We feel that the adverse publicity about you in *The Argos* . . .'

'It's all lies!' Mike snapped, vehemently.

'. . . and the unfortunate cruelty . . .'

'I told that bloody tick not to hit him!'

'. . . we thought it would reflect our high standards if we moved Welfare State back to his original yard . . .'

His eyes were friendly, as if bestowing a favour.

'. . . after all, we know what the problem is now.'

The bell rang for jockeys to be mounted. David Ware legged Mouse up on to Welfare State. Mike caught her eye. She smiled at him, half in apology, and allowed the horse to be led by one of Hugo's lads towards the entrance to the course. She had work to do.

Sandy 'n' Mandy were arm in arm with Hugo and David Ware, as they made their way towards the Stands, giggling excitedly.

Billy Dawson said, lamely,

'It's my job . . .'

Mike stared at him with contempt, then turned and walked away.

Black Deed was carefully prepared for the short journey in the box back to the yard. The bleeding had stopped. Travelling bandages were applied to his legs. His tail was wrapped. He was covered in a light cooling cloth, fastened by a surcingle.

Mike talked to him, reassuringly.

'You'll be all right, boy . . .'

There was no need to wait for their second runner. Welfare State would be going home in the Latimer transporter.

'Box him up, Joe,' Mike said, quietly to his Head Lad.

He walked out of the secure stable area. A small group stood waiting for him by the gate.

Frances, Kath Brant, John Grey and Pattie Roman surrounded him in silence as they headed for the car parks. Nobody said a word.

They heard the commentator drone. Then his voice raised in the closing stages of the race. One name clearly resounded over the course. Welfare State had won by six lengths.

John Grey's face did not alter.

They trudged along through lines of cars.

Scattered everywhere, they saw copies of *The Daily Gazette*, filled with smiling faces.

SIX

Black Deed looked well at the Sales. He was led by Mo round the auction ring, wearing a number on his bridle.

His reserve was only four thousand guineas.

There was little interest.

A small harassed-looking man in an old tweed jacket bid three five and then subsided into his catalogue.

Mike studied him, as the auctioneer tried to pump up another bid. He had not seen him for months.

Barry Ashwell was a close neighbour. His land adjoined Arkenfield's, three or four fields away. He had been a jockey. Now a trainer in a small way, specializing in the bottom end of the market. His owners were farmers and small businessmen whose hobby was racing. They kept horses fed, in warmth and comfort, with no chance of winning.

He was forty now, at least. He wore a gaudy tie, with the knot pulled low, showing the top button of his shirt. His cap was tipped forward, hiding his eyes. Once, he came third in the Derby.

There were no more bids.

James Brant turned to Mike, as they came out of the sale ring.

'Now what?'

Around them were owners, breeders and agents from

all over the world. It seemed as though every country was represented. Buyers, sellers and spectators from Australia, New Zealand, Japan, Ireland, France, South Africa, India, the Middle East and the United States, crowding into bars, carrying form books and catalogues, meeting old friends and rivals.

'There's one iron still in the fire,' Mike replied, enigmatically.

'Oh, come on. Everyone knows he's knackered. Didn't reach the reserve.'

Mo led Black Deed out of the ring, followed by Frances. They were hanging back, on purpose.

Barry Ashwell stood watching the horse, reflectively.

Mike caught his eye. He jerked his head towards the nearby bar and received a nod in acknowledgement.

'Excuse me, James —'

'Got to meet someone myself. See you later.'

Brant stalked off, so as not to be left standing. Mike walked over to Black Deed and patted him, reassuringly. Mo gave a little smile.

'Back in the box, Guv'nor?'

'Not yet. Leave him in the fresh air a bit.'

Mike took Frances by the arm, heading for the bar.

Barry Ashwell swirled a large whisky round his glass, ready to deal.

'Straight out with it, then. How much?'

'He's one of Mr Brant's, Barry. Not cheap.'

'Led out unsold, though.'

'You seemed to want him.'

Frances turned away, pretending to look to see if there was anyone in the bar she knew. She hated these unofficial bargainings. She spotted John Grey talking to an Italian in his own language.

'All right, put a figure on the table.'

Barry Ashwell sipped his whisky.

'Five and a half. Guineas,' Mike opened.

'Four.'

'I told you. He's one of Brant's.'

'Four two five.'

'No.'

'Bursting a blood vessel . . .?'

'Still decent. Might come yet. 'Scoped all right. I wanted to keep him, but Mr Brant's impatient.'

'I'll give you four and a half. Cash.'

'Four seven fifty. I've got to think of my owner.'

Ashwell glanced at Frances, but she avoided his eyes. He looked again at Mike, who stared back, serenely.

Ashwell sighed and stretched out a calloused hand. Mike shook it, formally concluding the deal.

'No names, no pack drill,' Ashwell said, quietly. 'Private sale. No commission, eh?'

Barry Ashwell drained his glass and stood up.

'Right. I've got a couple of others to look at . . .'

When he had left the bar, Frances asked sharply,

'What was the reserve?'

'Four. I hope it keeps James sweet.'

She looked at him disapprovingly.

'Black Deed's a crock, Mike. What about Barry?'

Mike gave a shrug. Who could tell? He had not been dishonest. Black Deed may have a question mark against him, but thoroughbreds were prone to blood vessel problems. The famous Herod had had the same weakness. Back in the eighteenth century, after a fine racing career, he sired more than a thousand winners.

*

Who could tell anything?

Everyone was an expert. Outside stable blocks, in paddocks and lunging rings, horses were being paraded before prospective owners. Youngsters who had not been named trotted up and down in front of appraising eyes.

'This the Arkana filly?' Mike asked a girl who was brushing a chestnut in one of the stable-boxes. She turned and nodded.

'Pull her out for me.'

Frances consulted her catalogue, looking doubtful.

'You're not thinking of this for James Brant, are you?'

Mike did not reply.

'Trot her up,' he said to the girl.

They watched as the filly trotted away and then back again, studying gait and action.

'Thanks, but no thanks,' Mike said.

The girl led the filly back into the box with a resigned expression to resume her grooming. She hated the business of selling.

Frances was puzzled. She walked along beside Mike as he looked at other animals, critically.

'Why the secrecy? Are you buying for someone else?'

Mike seemed not to hear her question. His eyes were intent on the horses.

James Brant met Peter Cassell, greeting him as an old friend.

'Peter, so glad you could make it.'

He was tall and silver-haired, still in his early forties. His lean face was lightly tanned against his white shirt. His dark grey suit had a discreet stripe and spoke of Savile Row. A red silk handkerchief was tossed artfully in his breast pocket. His black oxfords glistened.

Peter Cassell worked in the City of London.

There were others like him who worried James Brant. They worked in banks and institutions. They had various titles – fund managers, corporate accountants, investment analysts. He knew them by first names – Brian, Peter, Nigel, Harry. Each had the power to sanction or stop a twenty-million-pound deal in a moment.

Peter Cassell was an accountant who specialized in corporate affairs for a multinational firm of accountants. He was a partner representing an institution with a large block of shares in Brant's property company.

Brant did not want him as an enemy.

'My trainer's here somewhere. I'll introduce you. I'm sure you'll like him,' he said, charmingly.

He knew that Peter Cassell wanted to get into racing. That was one reason why he was there.

There was interest in a good-looking bay colt by Great Sasha out of Gads Hill. The sire was a sprinter, the dam a useful sort and the family tree had a few names in the black type of race winners.

Brant pushed his way through to Mike and Frances by the paddock rail, leaving Peter Cassell for a moment.

'This the one?'

Mike nodded, gloomily.

'Yes, but he's hardly a well-kept secret.'

'What are the chances?'

'Depends on your limit, James,' said Francis, matter-of-factly.

Brant was aware of the accountant approaching.

'Twenty,' he said, quickly.

'Dodgy.'

'All right, twenty-five, tops.'

He turned and beamed at Peter Cassell.

'Peter, I'd like you to meet Mike Hardy, my trainer—'

Mike shook his hand, smiled and turned back to the colt. He was too busy for pleasantries. Brant winked confidentially to Peter Cassell, and took him away to find a good seat.

The sale ring was bright with expectancy. The colt looked bold and confident and buyers saw a glittering future for him.

'. . . who'll start me at fifteen thousand guineas . . .?'

There was no response to the auctioneer. Other thoughts intruded into the minds of the buyers. Was that boldness a sign of weakness?

'. . . ten, then. Come on, I don't want to start any lower.'

A catalogue flicked.

'Thank you, sir. Ten thousand I'm bid . . .'

Mike sat next to Frances, who was bidding for James Brant. She made no move at first, then joined in at fifteen thousand. Mike tried to see who was against her. He spotted a man in a navy-blue blazer, signalling with the *Financial Times*.

'. . . fifteen-five. Sixteen. Sixteen-five. Seventeen.'

The auctioneer waited a moment.

'Seventeen in front of me. Seventeen-five anywhere? Selling at seventeen, then . . .'

Frances lifted her catalogue.

'Thank you. Seventeen-five. Eighteen.'

The man in the blazer topped every bid, relentlessly.

'. . . twenty-two thousand five hundred on my right. Twenty-three, sir? Twenty-three. And five. Twenty-four. And five. Twenty-five thousand guineas . . .'

Frances sighed as the limit was reached. James Brant

133

looked strangely submissive. He gave no sign of permission to continue. She sank down into her seat.

'. . . selling at twenty-five, then. All done?'

Mike suddenly raised his hand.

'Thank you. And five. Twenty-six.'

'Mike — what are you doing?'

Frances was surprised. She saw James Brant frown.

Mike ignored her and raised his hand again.

'And five. Twenty-seven. And five. Twenty-eight. And five . . .'

The man in the blazer slipped the *Financial Times* into his pocket.

'At twenty-eight thousand five hundred guineas on my right . . . No more? I'm selling at twenty-eight thousand five hundred guineas then . . .'

The gavel banged down.

'Mike Hardy,' the auctioneer said with finality.

Frances was annoyed. She thought Mike had exceeded his authority. Brant seemed to be hiding his face from them.

Mike left his seat and walked out of the sale ring, with Frances trailing after him, seeking an explanation

Outside, he shouted to Mo, who was hanging over the edge of the inspection ring, trying to glimpse the action.

'Mo!'

She ran over eagerly.

'Guv'nor?'

'It's ours. Get it ready to go home, quick as you like.'

Mo went to meet the colt as it was led out into the sunlight. It was a thrilling moment, the beginning of a new relationship. *

'James Brant is my client,' Frances said, sharply. 'What on earth do you think you are playing at?'

'Our client,' Mike corrected.

'What are you going to tell him? You've spent three and a half thousand over his top limit?'

Mike seemed unperturbed. He riffled his hand through his hair.

'James isn't my only owner . . .'

'You mean you've bought him for somebody else?'

Mike avoided answering her question.

'Could you give Mo a hand – while I sort out the paperwork?'

Black Deed and the colt were bandaged ready for travelling back in the old Arkenfield horsebox. Barry Ashwell helped to herring-bone them in, glad of the free lift.

'Why do it, Barry? Why buy other people's cast-offs?' Mike asked.

'My owners can't afford much. This one's won a race. Might raise the old image a bit. I've got two crackers at home they can't afford either, out of my old mare . . .'

Rich or poor, owners were a problem. There was no need to explain.

Frances spotted James Brant strolling towards them through the serried ranks of lorries and horseboxes. The accountant was no longer with him. Brant seemed to be enjoying a few moments of freedom, staring idly at horses bought and sold, lost in dreams.

She went up to him cautiously, dreading an outburst of anger.

'James, I'm very sorry about – '

'Not another word,' he said, pleasantly. 'What's three

and a half between friends? As long as he's not a wind-sucker, eh?'

Frances was surprised and suddenly realized her mistake.

'No. Mike went on to buy him for someone else . . .'

Pattie Roman lived in a Wiltshire cottage with an acre of woodland. She could work at her music without upsetting neighbours, hold noisy parties, or reflect in solitude. She found the peacefulness creative. She wrote songs and worked them into her repertoire.

Pete shared the house, but they were no longer lovers. The business they were building on her talent and his exploitation of it were much more important.

'You can't afford a racehorse,' Pete said, firmly.

Pattie sprawled on a sofa, dressed in an old sweater and jeans.

'Why not? I'm rich,' she joked.

'Successful. Rich isn't the same. There's the tax-man. Overheads. Me. Have you any idea of the cost?'

'Sell something,' she said, dismissing the subject.

He sat at a battered desk, working on his accounts. She was irresponsible and unmanageable.

'There's nothing to sell.'

The horsebox drew up outside Wellbourn Farm. The yard gate needed painting and hung from one hinge. The garden was overgrown. Weeds flourished between cracks and against moss-stained walls. Gutters and down-spouts were broken. Old machinery rusted in the hay-barn, and chickens ran loose in the yard. The old stables reminded Mike of the first day he took over Arkenfield, when it was still derelict.

Black Deed stepped carefully down the ramp, scenting the unfamiliar surroundings. Mo led him towards Gareth, a young stable lad with a cheery grin, who opened the gate with a practised knack to stop it scraping.

Barry Ashwell rubbed his hands and said to Mike,

'Thanks for dropping him off. Four-seven-fifty. Pounds, we said?'

'Guineas, come on. Four-nine-eight-seven and keep the fifty pence.'

'Right. Who do you want it making out to?'

'Cash, Barry. Do you want to pay my VAT as well?'

Barry Ashwell peeled one fifty-pound note from a crisp banded bundle and handed the rest to Mike.

'There's four-nine-fifty. I'll have to owe you the thirty-seven.'

Mike sighed and slipped the cash into his pocket. Mo climbed into the cab beside him and sat quietly, trying not to be sentimental.

'Aren't you going to count it?' Ashwell asked.

Mike laughed and started the engine.

'I live next door, Barry. Remember?'

The colt sniffed at his new Arkenfield home. His ears were pricked like an orphan. Other horses whickered a welcome. Mo walked him round the circular tack-room two or three times, praising and introducing him, before leading him into Black Deed's old box. The lads were excited – a new horse brought fresh hopes.

Later, Pattie Roman leant over the half-door and stared at him for a long time. Mike stood close beside her.

'Well, what do you think?'

'Big. Plenty of bone. Can I see him out?'

'You're the owner.'

'Pull him out, then.'

Mike stripped the summer sheet off and led him out of the box by his head collar. He paraded him round the yard for Pattie to see. She opened a packet of mints.

'He's called Garrynapeaka Lad.'

'What?'

'I think it's Irish.'

Pattie held out a mint on the flat of her hand. The big head reached forward and picked it up carefully with thick curling lips.

'I like him,' she said. 'He's called Garry . . .'

She argued with Pete on the telephone in Mike's office.

'Twenty-eight thousand five hundred. Guineas. One pound five pence. I don't know why. Tradition.'

'Plus VAT . . .' Mike pointed out, 'making thirty-five thousand –'

Pete slammed the telephone down.

Forms were filled in registering ownership, change of ownership and the Trainer's Authority to Act. Colours were chosen. Training fees were discussed. Pete did not ring back.

'Sell the car? Buy a moped?'

'Not mine to sell. Belongs to the company.'

Mike thought he might be faced with finding a new owner for Garry, and wondered how Brant would react.

'Pattie, haven't you got it?'

'Oh, just about . . .'

He thought she looked very beautiful.

'I don't want you to–'

She placed her hand on his, reassuringly. Her eyes were clear and her mind was made up.

*

138

Mike lay in bed thinking about Pattie Roman. It was midnight. He could not get to sleep. He had not met anyone like her.

He sensed danger in the attraction.

She probably had the same effect on thousands of fans. It was a quality of stardom.

Had Frances noticed?'

The feelings were vague but almost overpowering. He no longer trusted them. Signs of affection often pierced him with pain. A lover's look, a wife's warm glance at her husband, a father's smile.

He thought about Sally . . .

A warm glow entered the room.

Winter nights in front of the coal fire in the pretty cottage he lived in as Hugo Latimer's assistant, with Sally and Tom . . .

No! it was fire! He leapt out of bed and ran to the window, ripping the curtains open. The sky was red with flames.

He dived into his clothes and raced down the stairs.

Joe was already in the yard. It was bright enough to see. 'Where is it?'

They could hear sirens howling a mile away in the distance.

'Ashwell's place. We'd better get over there.'

They jumped into the Land-Rover and roared down the lane towards Wellbourn Farm.

It was a trainer's nightmare. The stables were ablaze. Horses screamed in terror. Hay-lofts were sheets of flame. A fire engine and three police cars blocked the yard. An ambulance waited outside, blue light whirling. Radio voices crackled loudly. Men were shouting. The gate was

open. Two panic-stricken wild-eyed creatures gallope
loose in the road.

'Bloody hell! Shut the gate!'

'It won't shut,' said a young policeman.

'Stop the horses!'

'I'm not stopping them. If they're out, they're fine
There's still some in there.'

The policeman knew nothing about horses.

'Joe, go back. Get the lads. Catch the loose ones.'

Joe drove off quickly. Mike heaved the gate across an
fastened it, cursing, then ran into the yard.

'Hey, you can't go in there . . .' the policeman starte
to say.

Firemen sluiced thousands of gallons of water over th
stable buildings, but the fire raged out of control.

Mike spotted Gareth in his pyjamas leading a mar
through the clouds of smoke. It was rearing and plungin
in pain. There was a stench of scorching hide.

'How many more?'

'Seven, guv'nor, all told. Three were out in the paddock
'Give me that. Where's Barry?'

Mike took hold of the rope which was tied to the mare'
head collar. Firemen and policemen stood back from th
flashing hooves.

'Trying to get the last one out . . .'

Behind them, part of the stable roof collapsed. The mar
bared her teeth and screamed. Mike was dragged acros
the yard, trying to hold her. The policeman at the gat
flinched as a thousand pounds of horseflesh ran toward
him. She saw the gate and checked, then turned aside t
run into the weed-choked garden in front of the farn
house, where Mike managed to bring her under some forr
of control.

140

Gareth fought his way back through the smoke. The stables were now a wall of flame. Firemen ordered him back. He took no notice, but the heat was too intense to get near. The rest of the roof fell in.

He saw a small shape huddled on the ground. It was Barry Ashwell, coughing and writhing in agony. His clothes were smoking. His hands and face were blackened and seared.

It took all night to round up the missing horses. The broodmare was taken to Arkenfield in distress. Two home-bred yearlings had somehow escaped. An eight-year-old gelding ran across a main road three miles away and was killed by a juggernaut. It was reported on the police radio.

'Seven horses. One's dead. We've got three. Where's the rest?'

Mike and the Arkenfield team searched until dawn. They combed the fields with flashlights. They drove up on to The Rudge and looked across black seas of open downland. They peered behind prehistoric barrow knobs and sarsen stones, high on the ancient tracks.

Just after daybreak, Mike found the two home-breds near Wellbourn Farm, under a tree at the far side of a field they had looked at in the dark. They were quietly eating grass.

The fire was out. The farmhouse was untouched, but the stables were gutted. Blackened timbers stood starkly in the rubble, drenched and steaming. The ambulance had gone. The fire engine and one of the police cars were still in the yard when Mike returned to check on the one horse still unaccounted for.

'It's dead, sir,' said the policeman, pointing to a large shape hidden beneath a tarpaulin.

Gareth had dressed and was standing nearby. He looked tired and stunned.

'Mr Ashwell's been taken to hospital. He's burned pretty bad . . .'

'I'm sorry, Gareth. I'll keep all the horses at Arkenfield for him. Which was the dead one?'

'That one the guv'nor brought back from the sales. The roof just fell in. I don't know what he was called . . .'

'Black Deed,' Mike said.

SEVEN

Her black skin was smooth and faintly musky in the half-light showing beneath the heavy, lined drapes.

Mike woke up at six, as usual.

A familiar headache throbbed behind his eyes and at the base of his skull like a drumbeat.

He had been drinking.

He stretched a hand out to kill the alarm before it rang. But there seemed to be more bed than there should be. He could not find the edge of it.

When he looked up, the ceiling was too far away. There was an ornate frieze he did not recognize.

He rolled over to one side, painfully. In the shadows he saw strange shapes which puzzled him. Something that looked like a table stood in the wrong place. He could make out the legs of elaborate chairs.

Where was he?

He tried to recall the previous day, but it had no pattern. His thoughts were scattered. For a few minutes he lay still and allowed unrelated images to float in his mind. He saw his father lying in the hospital ward, after the final stroke. He had said nothing for four days before dying but always seemed about to say something.

Mike remembered now that Barry Ashwell was in hospital in a burns unit and that Black Deed was dead. The sad eyes beneath Ashwell's head bandage reminded him of his father. The yard was ruined. Two horses were dead. The rented farmhouse was still intact, but the stable buildings were not insured. All Barry Ashwell owned now were the two home-breds and the brood-mare.

'Will you try and sell them for me?'

Barry had wanted to enter them in one of the big sales, like the Highflyer. He knew his owners couldn't afford them. But that would take time and a lot of preparation in a training yard.

Barry days as a trainer were over . . .

He could hardly survive before. His training fees were low. They just about covered the horses' keep. He had no Head Lad or skilled staff to help him. His owners sometimes delayed payment. He understood why and sympathized, but it meant that it was always a struggle. Dealing in horses was the only way he could make ends meet.

Mike saw the dreadful bulk of Black Deed under the tarpaulin which did not quite cover his feet. He had seen many dead horses unceremoniously winched up the ramp of the knacker's truck and taken away to be turned into dog meat.

He twisted around in the bed, trying to find a comfortable place for his head and saw a sleeping face next to his own.

Pattie Roman was naked beside him, under the crisp linen sheet.

He was shocked to see her, at first. Then he remembered the nightclub where she sang so beautifully, and the champagne.

He had refused to drink when Pete bought the first bottle the night before. They had sat together at a favoured seat listening to music, most of it jazz and blues, with occasional bursts of rock. There were other singers and groups, but Pattie was the star of the show. When she was on the floor, all conversation stopped and everyone listened for almost an hour. Mike had never heard her sing, even though he knew she had several best-selling albums. He had never seen her dressed and made-up like a black goddess, captivating everyone in the audience with song after song, one or two of which she had written herself.

'She's very good.'

'Don't tell her,' said Pete, 'she knows.'

Mike had been persuaded to go up to London by James Brant who wanted to impress an accountant. The sequence of events began to form as he realized where he was.

He was in a splendid Victorian hotel bedroom in Kensington.

Mike did not understand Brant, except as an ignorant horse owner and a benefactor who exacted a price for everything he gave. Horse-trading was the rule. At the sales he had vaguely seen a tall man in a dark suit who was introduced to him as Peter Cassell. Brant seemed anxious to please him. He wanted to find him a bargain. The best value Mike knew was represented by the two home-bred colts owned by Barry Ashwell. They gave him a good feeling as soon as he saw them. Frances had worked on their blood-lines with her computer-modem, accessing vast files of their ancestry.

Pattie Roman stirred in her sleep. Mike gently touched her black hair. He could not believe that he had made love to her. She seemed so strange and delicate, like a child. His hand was white against her face. She breathed easily and evenly. He wanted to kiss her, but did not move.

*

How did he get here? It seemed odd to find a woman lying beside him. Sally was the last woman he had spent a night with. There had been stable girls with whom he drank notoriously in the months after Sally had gone, but they were never there in the morning.

Sally Sherwood had been a stable girl when he married her . . .

He had not tasted alcohol for eight months. It was easy to think that the problem had gone. Those who had witnessed the crazy days of his drinking hoped that he had it licked. He now had orange juice or mineral waters with a dash of bitters. They no longer remarked upon it.

The rule was simple: stay away from the first drink, one day at a time. He had kept to it. But it was an invisible struggle. No one could see the hourly effort he made to conquer the craving.

One glass of champagne in a careless moment had led to this.

James Brant was fond of breakfast meetings, an idea he had grabbed in America years ago. Kath was disdainful, but he inflicted them on his colleagues whenever he could. They got the day off to a good start.

'Got a breakfast-meet with Peter Cassell. Remember?'

'Who?' asked Mike.

'That chap at the sales. Very important. Underline very. Can you get up to London?'

'For what time?'

'Eight o'clock sharp. Stay overnight. My expense.'

Mike had agreed. It meant making complicated arrangements, but he could not refuse. There were now five more horses to look after who only understood their own breakfast meetings. Mike had taken in all Barry Ashwell's homeless animals for the time being. But he was understaffed and although Gareth was doing his best, he was very slow.

Jack Ross offered to help. He was improving, but he was slow too, and Frances was worried that he might take the opportunity to get back in the saddle when no one was looking. She made him promise that he would restrict himself to feeding and mucking-out.

The critical meeting for James Brant, though, was at nine-fifteen in Fenchurch Street. It concerned an over-budget hypermarket, four months behind schedule. Penalty clauses were being invoked. All hope of profit had long ago disappeared and it was costing money by the hour. Peter Cassell would be sitting opposite him, along with a Nigel and a Brian.

Brant thought that a pre-business breakfast meeting would alter the tone of what threatened to be a disaster. He had assiduously cultivated Peter Cassell, who was a cold fish, and had discovered a common interest in racing. Using this opening, he had slowly built up a relationship. He had invited him to race meetings, along with others he sought to impress. So far, there had been no benefit from this because his horses had been disappointing. If only Mike understood how important it was for him to be seen as a winner.

Most of his colleagues simply enjoyed the day out. They did not mind backing a loser. But Brant did not want to appear to be a loser himself, by association. Only a fool would waste money training slow horses.

Peter Cassell had a wife who was bored. She started him thinking about buying a racehorse to give them a common interest. The horse-world and its characters excited her. With Brant's encouragement, it had slowly grown into an ambition and he visited the Sales.

At the breakfast meeting, Brant would offer him Barry Ashwell's home-bred colts. Both Mike and Frances had said they liked them. They were bound to be a bargain. Mike could enthuse in horsey-language and Peter Cassell would be impressed. If he bought one and put it in training at Arkenfield, they would share a bond. That could be useful . . .

Mike looked at his watch. The meeting was in an hour. His head ached and his throat was dry.

Pattie opened her eyes and smiled.

She had sounded thrilled when Mike said he would be in London for the night. She persuaded him to come to the club where she was singing.

'You can talk to Pete!'

'Who wants to talk to Pete?'

'Tell him all about Garry . . .'

Owners had others to please, usually. Trainers found themselves caught between spouses who disagreed. Constant disputes took place over horses. But it was the first time he had been asked to talk to someone like Pete.

As it happened, Pete was no trouble.

'How ya doing?' he asked when Mike sat down at the table.

'Good.'

Pete had an open bottle of champagne in an ice-bucket beside him.

'Fizz?'

'Not for me. Thanks.'

They discussed Garrynapeaka Lad briefly, before Pattie went off to get changed. He had worked on the gallops that morning. She was keen to know how it went.

'Looks like he'll stay.'

'How far?'

'Oh, I don't know yet. Let's give him time to settle.'

Pete sipped champagne and seemed to accept the inevitable with good grace, to Mike's surprise. His only mention of money came almost as a joke.

'Bloody great entry fees, vets, farriers, ho-ho. And the midgets who ride . . .'

Mike could not understand their relationship. He watched them for signs, but was baffled. When she had gone, Pete ordered more champagne. He poured a glass for Mike, catching the look in his eye.

'Don't worry. We're strictly business, nowadays. Cheers.'

She appeared in a single spotlight, looking magnificent. There were loud claps as she began to sing a favourite hit. Pete raised his glass to her in salute and Mike took a sip of champagne.

Mike had apologized to James Brant for buying Garrynapeaka Lad over his head, but he didn't seem to mind. He was more concerned about Black Deed. Mike had offered him the cash.

'He didn't want to pay commission on the deal. You aren't allowed to conduct a private transaction on the auctioneer's premises without giving them their cut.'

Brant refused to accept the money.

'Black Deed was still mine when he died. Officially.'

Mike suddenly saw the implications.

'I take it he was well insured?'

'Yes. Twenty thousand . . .'

Pattie kissed him. They fought playfully under the sheet, laughing, before making love again. Mike felt better.

*

Frances printed out all the lineage of the two home-breds. Mike had brought her the passports and papers from Barry Ashwell's office in the farmhouse kitchen.

'I'm going tonight,' he had said. 'Pattie's invited me to hear her sing. I'll go after evening stables.'

'Oh.'

She had covered up her fears, but Mike had added, 'Would you like to come?'

'No, I've got this to do. I gather it's top priority.'

She thought that Mike had looked relieved.

James Brant had asked for a thorough job as he could not risk a mistake with Peter Cassell. The accountant would check everything. The hypermarket figures were an example of his probing. Brant had not realized he was so far over budget.

Frances delivered them to his house later that night. There were points she needed to explain, back to the third dam and beyond. Thoroughbreds were all related. She showed him the significance of the print-outs which fascinated Brant. Barry Ashwell's home-breds were quite good.

He decided that Frances would be an asset at the breakfast meeting . . .

When they came out of the club after eleven, Pete hailed a taxi. Mike felt awkward standing next to Pattie. They had talked about eating somewhere, but Pete knew when he was not wanted.

'You two eat,' he said, 'I gotta call Melbourne. They want you to do some chat shows when you're over there.'

He climbed into the taxi.

'See you in the morning!'

The door slammed and the taxi pulled out into the traffic.

Mike and Pattie walked along the pavement to the next corner without saying a word. Then she grinned at him.

'Well?'

'What?'

'Your place or your place?'

The hotel restaurant was closed. The night porter suggested sandwiches in the room. Pattie asked for a bottle of champagne.

'Make it two,' she added.

'Not for me . . .'

'Don't be silly. We've got to celebrate.'

'What?'

'I gotta horse, remember?'

Mike showered and shaved. He peered at himself in the mirror. A bottle of champagne was nothing. One or two glasses of brandy. No one would know about his slip. He would pay the bill himself, so that Brant would not see. His eyes looked passable and his headache was getting better. He was not used to it, but it was a warning. Alcohol still had a frightening power over him. It would not happen again.

Pattie called out from the bed.

'What time's your meeting?'

'In ten minutes. Must be on time.'

'I hate working breakfasts. But coffee's a must.'

'You're going to join me?'

Mike was unsure. Pattie leapt out of bed. She still looked magnificent without her clothes.

'Just for the coffee . . .'

*

Peter Cassell walked into the dining-room at precisely eight o'clock to find James Brant drinking tea with a pretty young woman dressed in a suit. They sat at the best table, looking over the gardens.

'Good morning, Peter. This is Frances Ross. She's my bloodstock agent. Peter Cassell.'

'Good morning. I thought I was meeting your trainer?'

'Oh, he'll be along. Sit down. Tea or coffee?'

Brant was at his best, full of enthusiasm and confidence. He gave the impression of being a man in charge of life.

'What I think we may have here, Peter, is a great opportunity. Two first-rate horses for the price of one.' Brant laughed at his little supermarket joke. 'Well, not exactly. Frances will explain . . .'

Mike and Pattie were shown into the dining-room by the head waiter. They were half-way across the room when they spotted Frances. Had they thought of retreating, it was made impossible by Brant calling out,

'Mike! Come and join us!'

He was surprised to see Pattie, but instantly found an advantage in the situation. He stood up, beaming a welcome.

'Pattie Roman! Let me introduce you to Peter Cassell. Peter, this is Pattie Roman. I expect you recognize her. Pattie is one of our owners . . .'

Mike sat down opposite Frances. Pattie smiled at them all and poured herself coffee.

'Good morning,' Mike said, feeling embarrassed, 'I didn't expect to see you . . .'

Frances stared at him, not trusting herself to speak.

The breakfast meeting ended badly as well. Pattie Roman

left after five minutes of coffee drinking. She chattered about her horse and the cost of ownership. She mentioned guineas and value-added tax and extras and cheerfully said that she needed another hit to pay for it all. Then she kissed Mike on the cheek and departed.

Mike refused breakfast, drank tea and tried to answer Peter Cassell's questions honestly, but their tone irritated him. The first thing he wanted to know concerned ROC, which Mike did not understand.

'Return on Capital. I have to know what to expect.'

Mike illustrated the high-risk nature of racehorse ownership. He did not want to mislead the accountant, but he could see that he was not pleasing James Brant. He told the classic story of Snaafi Dancer, a son of Northern Dancer. He had cost record millions and was superbly bred, but he never raced and was useless at stud. There were no guarantees in racing.

James Brant tried to steer the conversation to the bargain home-breds, but Frances seemed to have lost the enthusiasm she had shown in his house the night before. The excitement had gone.

Peter Cassell probed into costs, capital costs and running costs, and grew more suspicious of the whole business.

'I don't think you think know how racing works, Peter.'

'Explain it to me.'

'You buy a horse. You pay me one hundred and sixty pounds a week, plus VAT, to train it for you. On top of that you pay extras, vet's bills, farriers, entry fees, jockey fees, presents for the lads and so much a mile transport to and from the races. That's the debit side.'

'On the other hand, these home-breds might win the Derby . . .'

James Brant wanted to lighten the mood. It was supposed to be a sporting man's meeting. Where was the laughter?

'Then retire to stud and make your fortune . . .'

He did not like the cold way Peter Cassell looked at him. Mike did not help.

'Or break down in training and end up as dog food.'

'I'm not a man who likes taking unnecessary risks . . .'

James Brant pushed his breakfast away, half-eaten. He looked at his watch, dreading the Fenchurch Street meeting.

The bloodstock insurance company agreed to pay twenty thousand pounds to James Brant for the loss of his horse. Barry Ashwell was given his money back. It turned out it was not his money. A greengrocer owner of his wanted to buy a cheap horse. He was still anxious to sell the home-breds.

James Brant decided to buy them, using the insurance money. He wanted to prove something to Peter Cassell, who had sided with Nigel and Brian after all. He asked Mike to get them as cheaply as possible.

Frances had suggested thirty thousand pounds for both of them.

Barry Ashwell sat up in bed, pleased to have a visitor.

'How are you, Barry?'

'Mustn't grumble, Mike. Good to see you.'

'Got a buyer for your colts.'

'Good work. Who?'

'James Brant.'

'Not cheap, eh? Surprise me.'

'Twenty.'

'Twenty for each, fine.'

'No, twenty for both, Barry.'

'I'm a sick man . . .'

'You need the money. Twenty's a fair price. How much do you want?'

'Fifteen each. That's about right.'

'Over the top. Twelve and a half.'

Barry Ashwell sank back on the pillow and sighed.

'All right. I can't shake your hand . . .'

Mike looked at the bandages and hated himself.

Pattie Roman kissed Garrynapeaka Lad on the nose. She gave him a mint. Pete sat in the Ferrari, listening to a tape, waiting for her. It was their last day in England before her tour of Australia.

'Look after him for me . . .'

She smiled at Frances, who was standing next to Mike in the yard. Mike was certain that she meant the horse.

EIGHT

Dangerous Lady was the best horse in the yard.

Mike knew that she would win a good race. Perhaps not one of the five great Classics which are the landmarks of the Flat Season – the One Thousand Guineas for three-year-old fillies, the Two Thousand Guineas for colts and fillies, the Derby in June, over one and half miles of the Epsom Downs, the Oaks, and the St Leger in the autumn.

But there were other good races in The Pattern. The Duke of Norfolk's Pattern of Racing Committee graded races throughout Europe into a system of three Groups, giving a series of races over the right distances for the time of year. This was to test and improve the constitution and soundness of the thoroughbred breed.

Group 1 were the Classics and the top European events, such the Prix de l'Arc de Triomphe or the Gold Cup at glittering Royal Ascot.

Group 2 had famous races like the Gimcrack at York, the Park Hill at Doncaster or the Jockey Club Stakes at Newmarket. Group 3 were important domestic preparatory contests, often called Classic trials.

Then there were Listed Races for good horses below Group standard, followed by a splendid variety of Handicaps, Maidens and Claimers. Flat races were run on more than half of the fifty-nine courses in the country.

Mike had to decide which race to enter The Lady in.

British racecourses are the best in the world. Green turf, watered by rain, left- and right-handed tracks, undulating ground, historic vistas. The tight left-hand oval of Chester, outside the Roman walls of the city, was written about as being raced over 'time out of mind' in 1512.

There were many considerations: the competition, the course, the going, the jockey and the conditions of the race.

The expression 'horses for courses' had significance. Some ran better left-handed, others right-handed. They performed their best at different distances. Some were sprinters, some stayers.

Dangerous Lady had speed but she was difficult to control and needed to be held back to conserve her strength for the run in.

Mike picked a race at Goodwood, towards the end of the season.

Mo claimed her weight allowance advantage as an apprentice female jockey and romped home at 10–1 on Raw Silk. It was not an important race, but she had stood in the Winner's Enclosure for the first time. She would remember the glorious feeling for the rest of her life.

She was part of Arkenfield now. She was a part of the magical racing world. She wanted to ride more and more winners.

Most of all, she longed to ride The Lady . . .

Evening stables finished at six. Half an hour before, the lads had everything ready for the Trainer's ritual inspection. Each horse was dressed over. Feet were picked out and greased, water buckets and hay-nets filled. Beds were set fair for the night.

Mike and Joe Hogan did the rounds of the boxes together.

Mo and the lads stood by their horses, ready to show them. Each 'did their two' or sometimes three. They took off the rugs and made them stand properly for Mike to see them at their best.

He felt their front legs for signs of heat or swelling in the tendons and joints. He checked for cuts. He asked questions about feeding and whether they were 'eating up' because a change in habits could be an early sign of something wrong.

Welfare State had been removed to Latimer's stable. Black Deed was dead. Chieftain's Son had been taken away by Tom Fisher. Vivid Dreams was winning races for the Brigadier with another trainer.

Rachael's Happy Brave continued to improve.

Three of Brant's string were useful: Fourcade, Blacksmith's Boy and Raw Silk. Four were hopeless rags.

Another group of owners, the Potter syndicate, had complicated shareholdings in two horses. They were good 'doers', which meant they ate their food, but they were not going to make a profit. Garrynapeaka Lad was still a new boy, and the home-breds were too young to assess. The other horses in the yard were never going to trouble the Judges.

James Brant owned only half of Dangerous Lady. It infuriated him that he needed the consent of the other shareholders before he could take a decision. Fifty-per-cent ownership gave him no control.

He blamed Kath for it. She should have known better

than to agree to Rachael's terms. If he only had fifty-one per cent . . . The Jockey Club frowned on ownership disputes. They could direct horses to be withdrawn from races until they were settled, or demand a public auction if they were not.

He suspected that Rachael had planned it this way.

Dangerous Lady had cost one hundred and forty thousand guineas. Guineas were gold coins minted in the reign of Charles II, 'the father of British turf', from gold imported from the Guinea coast of West Africa. In 1717 their value was fixed at twenty-one shillings. They were superseded a hundred years later by the sovereign. Racehorse prices were often stated in guineas, which were now £1.05.

The extra shilling on top of the pound made it £147,000.

Kath had committed Brant to pay half. Rachael split half of her half with the syndicate, keeping a quarter for herself. The other quarter was divided between John Grey and Frances Ross in the main, while Mike and Joe Hogan struggled to raise five per cent between them.

'Just about covered the bobs,' Joe had said.

The ownership details were registered with Weatherby's, the administrators of racing, in Northamptonshire. James Brant thought it very unfair that he had the largest individual stake, with no power at all to act. He began to think about how he could change this.

John Grey had taken fifteen per cent, for £22,050. As a gambler, his fortunes fluctuated. At the right moment, he could be persuaded to accept a good profit, which made Brant think that he could tempt him to part with his share.

Rachael would probably refuse. She did not have to please people like Nigel, Peter and Brian. A good filly like

The Lady, after winning a few races, could become a brood-mare for her.

Brant was wary about Rachael's relationship with Kath. They were, he suspected, talking about him behind his back.

Racing had once bored Kath, but now she was showing an interest. Since striking up a friendship with Rachael, she accompanied Brant more often. It was what he had hoped for, but she had become critical and questioned his decisions. Old feelings of inadequacy were stirred in him, which money did not cover. They should have had children.

Frances Ross had five per cent. He could not imagine changing her mind. She would tell Mike straight away, as well.

Mike and Joe Hogan shared five per cent between them. They must have had a lot of faith in The Lady to raise £3,675 each. Mike had no money that Brant knew of. He must have hocked everything.

Perhaps Dangerous Lady was the one good horse they were all searching for, the horse that could put Arkenfield on the map by winning a Group race soon. Brant could see himself standing as co-owner at Ascot, raising his black top hat and bowing.

The men in Fenchurch Street did not understand business. They only understood money. They could not run a toffee shop. When things were tight, as they were, they made demands and the tighter they became, the more demands they made. Business needed more money to survive a recession, not less.

The European funding for the cotton mill conversion was still stuck in Brussels.

He had not managed to prise it out of the interlocking advisory committees who each had a say in the awarding of grants.

Consultants had been busy for almost a year, charging by the hour.

The hypermarket was draining cash.

An executive housing development built on a landfill site remained only a quarter sold. Now methane gas was leaking from the ground.

A huge Japanese electronics company wanted to build an assembly plant on a green-field site. They were taking their time deciding upon which green field. Their management team were inscrutable. It was not even certain that he had won the contract.

His paper money had halved in value.

Peter Cassell had a rise in salary. He bought a quiet ten-year-old hunter for his wife to ride.

Brant savagely hoped she would fall off.

One morning Mike had a telephone call from a very polite-sounding young woman to make an appointment for an early-morning visit to the yard for herself and her employer.

They arrived as First Lot were pulling out.

Mike was impressed by the dark-green Rolls-Royce whispering up to the gate at seven o'clock, a uniformed chauffeur at the wheel. A small man in a Herbert Johnson tweed hat and a Burberry raincoat sat in the back, with a beautiful black-haired girl besides him. She looked very young, about twenty. She got out first and introduced herself to Mike.

The tiny man emerged from the car, took off his hat and bowed low.

'This is Mr Akiro Mishima,' said the girl.

Mike bowed low in return. They were all Japanese.

Akiro Mishima could not speak English. The girl told Mike that she was his interpreter in England and France. She had dark mellow eyes. Her voice sounded light and affectionate. Perfect white teeth shone when she smiled.

'Mr Mishima would like to watch the horses – exercise?'

Mike drove them up to the gallops in the Discovery, Mr Mishima sitting hunched in the back staring out over the Downs, saying nothing.

The interpreter's name was Kiko. She explained that Mr Mishima was an important thoroughbred owner in Japan. He had won many cups and wanted to have a second string in Europe, as his company needed him to spend more time in England. They would be building an assembly plant soon.

He planned to run the best horses on both sides of the world in the top races.

He needed a small training yard in Berkshire, near Heathrow Airport, close to the new plant. His company was searching for a suitable site in the area.

But which did he want to find first?

Mr Mishima watched 'work' for the full hour.

The horses in training had a routine. Two easy days when they only walked or trotted near the stables, alternated with two canter days and two 'work' days when they galloped. On Sundays they stayed in.

Mo rode by on Dangerous Lady at full gallop. She was showing off, wanting to impress Mike with her growing skill as a jockey.

Mr Mishima's eyes lit up as he watched her. He spoke to Kiko excitedly.

'He is pleased with your brown horse,' she relayed to Mike. 'He says he has not seen a better one in all the stables we have looked at.'

'Is that true? Would he liked to see more?'

Mr Mishima continued talking.

'What name is the horse?' Kiko asked.

'Dangerous Lady. She's a bay filly.'

He saw Mr Mishima nod, as she tried to translate.

'He has seen enough, thank you, Mr Hardy.'

'Then I'll take you back and show you the yard.'

James Brant was there when they got back. He appeared to know Mr Mishima and they bowed to each other politely.

Mike was annoyed at the way Brant took over and conducted the tour. He felt as though he was being excluded, hearing Mr Mishima laugh at Brant's jokes as Kiko translated them.

The builders were starting on the conversion of an outbuilding into a laboratory, for Mike believed that the daily testing of blood would help to assess a horse's condition. He was keen to explain his theories to Mr Mishima, but James Brant kept him too occupied with jokes.

Ten minutes later, they were bowing again.

When the Rolls-Royce had gone, Mike complained angrily,

'You did that on purpose!'

James Brant remained calm.

'I did what?'

'He's an important prospect. He's looking to place a string in an English yard. I didn't need your interference!'

'Who do you think sent him to Arkenfield . . .?'

Mike was suddenly silent.

'But I called in to ask you to look at a horse . . .' Brant continued.

He led the way to the office, explaining that he had heard of a colt for sale in Ireland. Mike did not take it all in, at first.

'You know Sean Joyce? The Man?'

Everyone in racing knew The Man. He was a legendary Irish bloodstock agent . . .

'Of course I do.'

'Well, it's there in his field.'

Buying a horse from a field, training it and seeing it win was the stuff of racing dreams. They could always come true . . .

'I've asked Frances to go for me. You could go along as well. Joe can look after things for a few days.'

'Me? Go to Ireland?'

'I think it could be very important . . .'

Mike was not sure what to say.

The Rover, with Frances at the wheel, held a steady eighty-five. She had been late picking him up. Mike sat next to her, glancing crossly at his watch.

'It doesn't take off until half past. We'll make it.'

She was unruffled.

Mike could not spare the time away from Arkenfield. The Lady needed preparing for her race at Goodwood.

Garrynapeaka Lad had an outing, Fourcade was as lame as a cat, the builders were there and Rosie the Dragon was off sick. Joe Hogan had been left in charge of everything.

Jack Ross had offered to help out again.

'Don't worry about the yard,' he said. 'If Sean thinks it's worth a look, it must be special.'

Frances slowed down and moved into the inside lane of the motorway as the signs for Heathrow came up.

Mike really did not want to go to Ireland, and was angry with himself for letting James Brant persuade him, but Brant had insisted that it was important for the yard's future.

Frances was longing to meet The Man, as his fame had reached Kentucky where he visited the big Keeneland Sales. He had the uncanny gift of being able to pick very good animals where others missed them.

She had jumped at the chance to look at his colt, but she worried about leaving her father at Arkenfield. A strong feeling of foreboding came over her. She knew that he would be tempted to ride in her absence.

Mike's temper did not improve.

The Aer Lingus plane touched down an hour late at Shannon. The hire car was lost in the compound and it was raining. Frances did not want her portable computer to get wet.

When they got on the road at last, Mike took a wrong turning in Limerick and wasted another twenty minutes. Frances sat with a map, giving directions. She had arranged for them to meet Sean Joyce at five o'clock in the Shannon Hotel, Kilgunbally.

They stopped in Abbeyfeale to look at the map again. Frances wanted a cup of tea.

'We're two hours behind already,' Mike snapped furiously.

'We go left here over the Glanaruddery Mountains to Castleisland. Then on to the Atlantic.'

The tyres hissed in the rain as they moved off, chased by a barking dog.

The Shannon Hotel faced the ocean on the cliffs of County Kerry. Although it did not live up to its grand-sounding name, it was nonetheless very popular. It had seen better days. The wind-lashed front needed painting, the woodwork was stripped bare by salt, but it was the focal point of the small stone town.

The rain had finally stopped. A mackerel sky glowed in the setting sun as they stopped outside, and the ocean shimmered vast and golden.

The hall was warm and welcoming. A large, strikingly handsome woman in her fifties greeted them at the reception desk.

'Good evening. I'm Deirdre Ryan. May I help you?'

She had a soft Irish lilt and pronounced her name Deirdra. She was the widowed owner of the hotel and Frances took to her immediately.

Mike had not lost the sharp annoyance in his tone all day.

'My name is Hardy. Mr Joyce is expecting me.'

'Who?'

'Sean Joyce, the bloodstock agent.'

'There's no Mr Joyce staying here.'

'I didn't say he was. I said he's expecting me – at five o'clock!'

Deirdre Ryan looked round at the long-case clock behind her. It showed seven o'clock.

'You're a little bit late. But he's not here. So it doesn't matter, does it?'

Jack Ross rode back from the Downs on Mike's steady

166

ten-year-old hack, Nelson. He had not allowed the horse to canter, but posted gently in a rising trot, feeling the weakness in his knees. Strength would come back in time. He just needed practice.

Mo and the lads were lined up for evening stables when he got back to Arkenfield.

A dark-green Rolls-Royce stood outside, beside James Brant's car.

Mr Mishima followed Joe on his round of the boxes, asking a lot of questions which Kiko tried to translate.

Joe had objected when James Brant arrived, saying that Mr Mishima wanted another look at the yard.

'Rather he came back when the Guv'nor's here . . .'

'Why? We've got nothing to hide.'

Brant winked at Joe and added in a low voice, 'I think the idea is to catch you on the hop. See the place warts and all before making a decision . . .'

'I get it,' said Joe, catching on.

He turned to the interpreter.

'Feel free to look at whatever you want.'

Mr Mishima was interested in every detail. Kiko found difficulty with the terms, in her own language as well as English.

When they reached Mo, who was standing with Dangerous Lady, Mr Mishima bowed to her. She giggled with embarrassment, but he showed great respect for her as a horsewoman and asked her to walk the filly around for him. As she did, proudly, his eyes glinted and his head nodded appreciatively.

The Lady was sleek, glossy and magnificent.

*

Mike used the pay phone, but could not get through to any number he had for Sean Joyce.

They had arranged to stay the night at the Shannon.

'Would you like a double or a twin-bedded room?'

Frances wanted to know if there was another hotel instead.

'No . . .'

'Then two singles – preferably on different floors,' she said, seeing Mike banging the telephone in frustration.

Deirdre Ryan nodded, understandingly.

Mike rang Arkenfield and left messages on the answering machine. He tried other numbers, but could not get John Grey or Rachael, so he rang the Dog and spoke to Nick who said Joe was not there. Mike could hardly hear over the background noise in the bar, but he gathered that James Brant had brought Mr Mishima to Arkenfield again.

He tried James Brant's numbers, without success. Kath had no idea where he was.

Sean Joyce did not reply when Mike rang him again.

Frances sat in the dining room next to the bar, beginning to feel miserable.

'Your coffee's in the lounge, Miss Ross – in front of the fire.'

'Thank you, Mrs Ryan.'

'I'm known as Deirdre, or the Widow Ryan. I prefer Deirdre.

'Thank you, Deirdre.'

Frances followed her, passing Mike, who was still trying to make contact on the telephone in the hall.

'Your man has a lot on his mind . . .'

'He's impossible!'

Next morning they decided to drive South over the mountains to the stud at Ballinadare and got lost again. It seemed as though the signposts were twisted round the wrong way. Rainclouds gathered round Macgillycuddy's Reeks.

Mike stopped the car by a bridge to give Frances a chance to find the river on the map.

'Have you any idea where we are?'

'Yes!' said Frances, quickly.

'Good.'

'Vaguely . . .'

He reversed in a temper, spinning the wheels on the gravel. He had seen a road leading off the main road which might give them another reference point.

The nearside rear tyre punctured and collapsed on to the rim.

Mike gripped the steering wheel and stared ahead through the windowscreen as the rain began to fall.

'Mike . . .'

'What?'

Frances hesitated.

'My computer . . .' she said, nervously, 'I've left it at the hotel.'

At Newbury John Grey was telling Rachael that James Grant had asked him how he felt about making a profit on the sale of his fifteen per cent share in Dangerous Lady.

They were sitting in the Owners' and Trainers' bar, waiting for the start of the second race. Garrynapeaka Lad was not expected to be in the frame. It was raining and the going had changed.

'He asked me the same thing,' said Rachael.

'You think he's got a buyer lined up?'

'There's nothing he can do without our agreement.'

They stayed inside and watched the race on the closed circuit television. Garry was tailed off.

Later they spotted James Brant and Kath coming into the bar with a large powerful man in his sixties, wearing a light Donegal tweed suit.

Rachael waved to Kath. She smiled and came over, as her husband ordered the drinks.

John Grey's face changed.

She followed his gaze, but she did not recognize the genial, sun-reddened face next to James Brant in the crush.

'Who's that?'

John Grey stood up to get more chairs.

'He is The Man,' he said. 'His name is Sean Joyce . . .'

NINE

The Man bought and sold young, well-bred horses.

His clients were among the richest people in the world. The rare gift he had of divining which horse to choose was well rewarded.

His name was kept on a secret list in Windsor Castle. Wall Street bankers paid highly for his opinion on foals and yearlings. Arab sheikhs trusted his advice and began to find winners after their early expensive mistakes. Japan and Hong Kong were eager to find the finest animals in their growing passion for racing and breeding.

Sean Joyce was sixty-five years old. He called himself a horse dealer, not a bloodstock agent, and viewed computer-generated analyses of bloodlines with caution. Given good breeding, the merits of horses were assessed by hand and eye.

He looked at them. He felt their tendons and bone structure with hands that seemed to know more than most. He had studied the champions of forty years, and had quietly influenced the decision to buy many of them.

He lived with his wife Aileen in a stone farmhouse in a remote part of Kerry, in the south of the Republic of Ireland. Roads leading to it were hilly, narrow and winding.

He had good reasons for choosing this hidden valley.

Running freely in the bright green fields outside his window were dozens of very young thoroughbreds, eating rich Irish meadow-grass and drawing into their developing lungs pure air, driven by the Atlantic westerlies across three thousand miles of open ocean.

They could not be locked away in safes or bank vaults. But these horses represented large investments to their different owners, who patiently waited for them to grow into racing machines.

Horse-stealing thrived on the closeness of main roads and motorways. A box or a closed truck could vanish in a few minutes.

Sean Joyce's horses were well protected by wandering Irish miles of impenetrable lanes with no signposts.

Joyce preferred to meet visitors in the Shannon Hotel. Then, if he pleased, he would drive them out to the farm in his Range Rover. It took over an hour by the tortuous short cuts, and by the time he turned in through the unmarked gates at the edge of his hundred acres, they were usually lost, confused or disorientated.

But yesterday, James Brant had peremptorily cancelled The Man's five o'clock meeting with Mike Hardy and Frances Ross at the Shannon Hotel.

Instead, he had asked him to come to England to look at a filly for Mr Mishima, stressing urgency.

Joyce took the first available flight to Heathrow.

He had been retained by Mr Mishima since picking him the winner of the Japanese St Leger.

The Man thought that Dangerous Lady was a possible.

Mr Mishima had bought two possibles in Ireland, one in England and one in France. He wanted two more to make up his first European team, and planned to test them in the competitions of Britain, Japan and the Far East.

When Sean Joyce described a horse as a possible, its value increased dramatically. A frown on his genial brow caused many hopes to weaken, and if he walked away, they were dashed.

James Brant had taken a huge risk telling Mr Mishima about The Lady. They began to talk about horses, through his interpreter, as a welcome topic of common interest in a whole world of differences.

The assembly-plant contract was mired in endless, baffling negotiation. Japanese protocol was incomprehensible. They were stalling, Brant thought.

But he needed a quick decision, desperately.

His company was threatened. A new project would regain some credibility in the offices of Fenchurch Street.

Mr Mishima was surprisingly keen to see the horse Brant had zealously described as a potential Classic winner and, instead of formal politeness, his attitude changed to warmth.

He discussed the deficiencies of calcium and other minerals in the grass of Hokkaido and the seven Derby winners Japan had imported to improve their breeding stock. He seemed to be more interested in Tokyo's new international race than the new buildings.

Yet formerly insuperable obstacles to agreement, in the terms and conditions of the contract, were cleared away in a few hours, when once they had caused months of delay.

Mr Mishima wanted to be given the opportunity to look at Dangerous Lady, with a view to buying her.

*

A preliminary inspection had taken place under the pretext of a tour of Arkenfield.

Mr Mishima was seeking a home for his new string and had agreed to the small deception. He knew how sensitive trainers were to a change in the ownership of their best horses. More often than not, in every country, it meant their removal to another yard.

He was very excited indeed by what he saw on the Downs. If Sean Joyce, the agent he relied upon, approved of his choice, he would offer £500,000. James Brant did not see how he could refuse.

He knew that Mike would not agree. Dangerous Lady was his big hope for the future. He suspected that John Grey could be tempted, but Rachael would persuade him against it. Frances would support Mike.

A simple idea formed in his mind, which required him to get rid of Mike for a few days.

Then The Man could visit the yard and see the filly, without raising any immediate suspicions.

And it would give Brant the chance to break the weakest link in the ownership syndicate, with no interference from Mike or the other shareholders. They would all profit anyway.

He would stun Joe Hogan with a generous bid for the two-and-a-half per cent he held. That would gain him the majority shareholding and control of the destiny of the filly, at the least direct cost.

Joe Hogan turned down his offer of ten thousand pounds.

James Brant had given him a bottle of single malt whisky.

'I'll talk it over with the Guv'nor – when he gets back.'

'No time for that, Joe. The Man wants a result.'

Joe Hogan had bought his stake with most of his savings for £3,675, in the hope that he would back a winner at last.

Since his first paltry wage packet as a stable lad of fifteen, he had placed money on horses, in singles, doubles, yankees and accumulators and was still chasing his losses.

The Lady would win a good race soon, and Joe would be part of her glory and Arkenfield's success.

He felt unfairly trammelled by gambling, beer, and a wife with strong ideas of her own who had left him to waste his money a long time ago.

He swigged the Scotch without savouring it, and argued with himself.

As far as he could see, it would make no difference to anyone if he thought of old Joe for once . . .

He said he would take fifteen thousand.

Mike changed the wheel in the rain. He and Frances drove back to the Shannon Hotel to pick up the portable computer she had left behind.

Deirdre Ryan showed them how to get to Sean Joyce's farm on a large-scale map behind a glass case in the hotel office. Frances took notes, because the web of country lanes were not marked on her tourist guide.

There were no telephone messages.

When they set off again, Mike apologized for his temper.

'It's just the worst time to be away. The Stakes are in two weeks and I want The Lady right.'

'You must learn to delegate. Trust people.'

Mike looked at her dourly and swerved to avoid a caped figure on an old bicycle who turned right without warning.

They arrived at the unmarked gate in the afternoon. The rain had finally stopped. Frances was sure that the twin narrow tracks with grass growing in between led to Sean Joyce's farm. They bumped along over drainage channels and rattled across cattle-grids, through four field-gates.

A rainbow curved up from behind the barns of the stone house in the valley.

Aileen Joyce calmed two red setters and a fierce mongrel as she explained that her husband was away in England, across the water.

'We've come to see a horse,' Frances said, trying to hide her disappointment.

'Which one would that be?'

They counted thirty young horses in the fields and paddocks near the farmhouse, and saw more beyond. Aileen Joyce had no idea which one was for sale.

Jack Ross rode Mike's twelve-year-old hack over the cavalletti jumps in the schooling ground which were set low.

He had ridden Nelson in steeplechases five years before and knew there was no danger. Nellie was an armchair.

He presented the horse to the first expertly, but felt an excruciating shock of pain in both his legs at the sharp impact of landing on the other side. It unsettled him, and his misjudged the stride at the next.

Mo and Nick watched as Jack fought to hold his balance.

Nelson sensed the change in his rider's rhythm and hesitated. Jack gripped with his legs, but the power in them had gone.

His heels were wedged in the irons. He braced himself for the small obstacle as if facing the challenge of a huge fence at Aintree, leaning forward, flowing, letting the horse rise beneath him.

But he twisted with agony when Nelson stumbled slightly on landing.

He lost his seat, slipped off sideways and tried to roll into a ball. He felt the crack as he hit the ground face down.

Mo and Nick dashed to where he lay huddled, groaning in torment.

Rachael found the big, bluff Irishman fascinating.

John Grey introduced them in the racecourse bar and Sean Joyce's easy charm drew her at once.

He reminded her of Frank. They would have been about the same age. The Man had humour and confidence, just like her husband, and they both had a deep knowledge of horses. She was still trying to acquire a fraction of it.

Powerful fearless men who had life by the throat – she thought they could never die.

She was delighted to hear that Sean Joyce had known her husband well, through many friends in Kentucky. He had stories to tell about him that she hadn't heard. The way he spoke brought memories flooding back, but Sean Joyce made them all seem happy and funny. He accepted death in a natural way and banished grief and regret to sulk in a corner.

Rachael felt uplifted.

James Brant, however, seemed preoccupied and did not join in the conversation. The Man roared with laughter at his own amusing recollections. He ordered champagne and began to seem like a party.

They decided to adjourn to the Oast House after the last race.

Kath was disappointed that she couldn't go with them. Brant had invited some business colleague to dinner in a pretentious restaurant she didn't like, and wanted her support. A Peter Cassell and his wife Carol. She was not looking forward to it.

Irish dance music filled the Shannon Hotel.

Mike and Frances returned despondently that evening from their fruitless journey to Sean Joyce's farm, and found an odd assortment of men and women, some well into middle age, gathered in the hall. The men were spruce in newly pressed suits, their shoes glistening with polish, while the ladies sparkled in costume jewellery and brightly coloured dresses – soft silks, floating chiffon, and flattering summer florals. An over-exotic mixture of scents hung in the air.

They stood in a line by the entrance to a big room with an open expanse of sprung wooden floor, in need of renovation.

A cheerful ceilidh band tried to entice them in with familiar, foot-tapping reels, but the men hovered uncertainly, trying to decide which of the ladies to ask to accompany them, summoning courage.

They were all single, looking for partners.

Deirdre Ryan, immaculate in black satin, made suitably pleasing introductions. Couples shyly took to the floor and they danced formally, as the music became more intimate.

The Widow Ryan was a trusted matchmaker.

She smiled when she spotted Mike and Frances as they looked on bemusedly.

'Miss Ross and Mr Hardy, welcome. We have a little dance tonight. There's been a telephone message for you from England.'

'Oh, yes? Who from?'

'Mr James Brant. He said to apologize for sending you

here on a wild-goose chase. There'd been a last minute change of plan. He couldn't get hold of you . . . You're to stay over until the morning.'

After the X-rays Jack Ross was strapped in a St John sling in the casualty ward at the hospital. He had injured his shoulder and broken his clavicle.

Rather than wait for an ambulance, Nick and Mo had driven him there in the back of the old Land-Rover. A fall on the Downs involved a longer delay before the portable telephone cut the need for the long dash to summon help.

Jack insisted that he did not want Frances to be told. She would find out soon enough when she came back from Ireland.

James Brant haggled. He finally agreed to pay Joe twelve thousand five hundred pounds and made out a cheque. Joe stared at it with mixed feelings.

He knew that neither he nor Mike had any power against the whims of the major shareholders. Their combined holdings were only five per cent.

He had bitter experience of a lot of good things in the past – gold-plated winners beaten a bus ride, horses that broke down in training, or on the track, multiple bets which collapsed on the final race.

This was a certain win. He tried to tell himself that there was no harm in accepting it.

'But I want the papers signed and Weatherby's informed first thing in the morning,' said James Brant, shaking his hand.

'All right, Mr Brant. Done.'

Joe slipped the cheque into his inside pocket. Later, he went to The Dog and got drunk.

But he told nobody. He was not celebrating.

The Man did not discuss his clients' affairs or the price
they paid for horses, but kept their secrets as close as a
priest. So it was hard for John Grey to find out about
what was going on, when they talked over dinner in the
Oast House.

They ate an excellent meal, drank good claret with it
and talked about everything else.

Rachael, who was with them, was not interested
anyway. She reminded John Grey that there was nothing
James Brant could do. If he wanted to sell the Lady, he
would have to get their consent and they would simply
refuse to give it. She wanted to hear more about Frank.

But from the corner of her eye, she thought she saw the
faint flicker of a frown cloud The Man's brow . . .

Deirdre Ryan had given them different rooms. They were
now adjacent on the same floor and Mike could hear
Frances running a bath.

He had spent more time on the telephone, without much
success. Everyone seemed to be out. He cancelled the seat
on the 10.15 flight that evening, and checked on the next
day's bookings.

Mike was frustrated and annoyed. He could not rid
himself of the feeling, which had been with him since
leaving Arkenfield the day before, that he was being
manipulated by James Brant. But he could see no reason
that made sense. Perhaps it was all the fault of the madden-
ingly carefree Irish, who had so little respect for time.

He had watched Frances talking to the Widow Ryan in
the hall while he made his calls. They seemed to be in

league in a conspiracy, talking and laughing as if they had been friends for years.

He felt guilty about Frances.

His bad temper had spoiled what should have been a pleasant trip and a good opportunity to mend fences. It had maintained a distance between them. She had not mentioned his night with Pattie Roma and her attitude puzzled him. But there were too many places where they could hurt each other. If he had the words, he could try to explain that Pattie Roma had given him a moment of freedom, how liberated he had felt from a turmoil of conflicting emotions which he did not understand. The champagne had helped him escape.

But it would never happen again. He knew that he could not keep up with the black singer. He was probably history already, like Pete.

There was no reason for him to be defensive. Since that night in London, he had hidden behind a brusque businesslike manner that had not allowed Frances room to approach him.

He could hear her singing an Irish ballad in the bath-room.

Later, when she came down the stairs to join him in the hall, he was astonished. She wore a black sheath dress, cut very low, her hair was shining and high-heeled shoes seemed to transform her figure. She looked elegant and graceful.

He was used to seeing her in jodhpurs and boots, or an old raincoat. Sometimes she wore a suit, or a practical blazer and skirt.

'You look terrific,' he said.

'Shall we dance . . . ?'

She led him protesting towards the entrance to the ball-room.

'I can't. I was born with two left feet. I'm useless.'

'Then I'll dance with an owld farmer,' she laughed.

Deirdre Ryan nodded at them, a small smile playing on her lips, as Mike took Frances in his arms.

The band were playing 'Casey would waltz with his strawberry blonde . . .' as they joined the other couples on the floor.

Kath was bored. She tried to talk to the horsey woman with big teeth who sat opposite her at the dinner table. Carol had a son who was being interviewed for a university place and an incorrigible daughter at Roedean. Kath of course had no children to discuss. Carol had just been bought a horse to ride called Horse, which she thought was most amusing.

Peter Cassell and her husband were ignoring them. They did not seem to be enjoying themselves. Kath heard odd snatches about a Japanese contract, penalty clauses, share prices and large sums of money.

She made another gallant attempt.

'How interesting! Tell me all about Horse . . .'

The Man ordered a taxi to take him to the Excelsior.

Rachael was sorry to see him go as she had enjoyed his company enormously. They had talked about Frank as a breeder and she learned that Sean Joyce had thought highly of him. She wanted to discuss one of her stallions, who was not performing his duty, and she had a thousand more questions whirling in her mind. She was creating a living memorial to Frank and wanted to make his stud a success but there still too many things she did not understand.

She asked about Frank's first wife, but The Man offered no criticism. He seemed to see good in everybody.

So it came as a shock when he said,

'Shame about his son David, though. A wrong one there.'

Rachael wanted to know more, but he quickly changed the subject.

By then, it was late and The Man was ready to leave. He wanted to catch the first flight back in the morning.

John Grey had tried everything he could to find out more about Dangerous Lady and James Brant, but he was no wiser. He paid the bill, feeling uneasy.

'Don't worry,' said Rachael, over a last brandy.

They sat in silence for a long time, looking at each other. The other diners had drifted through to the bar and waiters were clearing tables, pointedly.

John Grey eventually made the connection. 'Joe Hogan,' he said suddenly.

Mike and Frances were lost in another age. The music was soft and dreamlike. The mood was set. Lights were dimmed. Dark figures clasped together in a slow romantic waltz.

They felt passions and yearnings all around them.

There were no words. Only sentimental strains, warm fragrances and the embrace of willing arms.

Mike wanted to kiss her.

He had lost the awkwardness of his faltering steps in the first few dances. Other men were just as bad, clumsily reading on toes.

Burly farmers towered above birdlike women. Giants blundered in the two-step and jigs before dinner. A delightful group of children dressed in green velvet had danced a hornpipe, with straight backs and serious eyes.

Men and women were drinking, but Mike refused. Frances had a little white wine.

They held each other.

Mike and Frances felt spellbound in the galaxy of loneliness and need that revolved with them around the floor, in the flickering shadows.

Frances looked up at him.

They kissed with deep mutual longing.

In the darkness, there were other kisses and the Widow Ryan was well pleased.

After the last dance, they walked together on the shore, saying nothing, as the white horses rolled in. They kissed again in the moonlight.

Then they turned back to the hotel, their arms locked tightly, and went inside . . .

The next morning, Joe Hogan's head felt like an anvil with the blacksmith hammering on it. He walked across the yard towards the office.

Mo Ratcliffe looked down from her seat on The Lady, circling the yard after First Lot.

'Joe? When the Guv'nor starts thinking about a pilot, you'll put in a good word, won't yer?'

'What?'

'The Stakes. I can do the business.'

'For cryin' out loud,' said Joe.

He turned to see John Grey's blue Alvis standing in the entrance alongside James Brant's white BMW. Rachael Ware's Range Rover was just turning in. Joe knew he must face a Stewards' Enquiry.

'I've changed my mind, Mr Brant.'

'You can't do that! We shook hands!'

Joe handed the crumpled cheque back, now as valueless as a losing betting slip. One look at the faces of John Grey and Rachael had told him that he had made a mistake.

'I'll double my offer,' said James Brant.

'You mean twenty-five thousand . . . ?'

Joe could hardly bear to hear his own voice, turning it down. He turned to John Grey. Another gambler would understand.

'It's not the money, Mr Brant . . .'

'What is it, then?'

'I didn't know you were going to sell The Lady to Japan. I couldn't do that, not to the Guv'nor.'

When he had seen Sean Joyce in the yard, Joe had suspected something. But it had taken a while to make the leap.

James Brant saw the expression of fellow-feeling on John Grey's face and decided to strike him.

'You know what you're turning down, John? Half a bloody million. If we sell, your share will add up to seventy-five grand.'

Rachael waited. She could get one hundred and twenty-five thousand, but she wanted to keep The Lady.

John Grey stared at Joe and thought hard.

'Well?'

The change of ownership documents were laid out on Mike's desk. They all knew that The Lady was entered at Goodwood. Through the window, they saw her quietly strutting round the yard, with Mo patting her neck.

The office was quiet, with Rosie away.

The Lady was their one good horse. They could decide to sell her without Mike and Frances being able to stop them.

But John Grey said nothing.

TEN

Goodwood, high on the chalk Sussex Downs, near Chich-ester, is sixty-five miles from London.

It is the most beautiful racecourse in England.

Laid out by the third Duke of Richmond, on a part of his estate, the right-handed track undulates over rolling greensward.

Glorious Goodwood used to mark the close of the London 'season' in the nineteenth century. The meeting at the end of July combined top-class racing, on its dips and rises, with an important social occasion.

It was the summer Ascot, without the formality. There were no top hats and tails — it was panamas and sports jackets, sundresses and casual clothes, strawberries and cream.

Mo Ratcliffe would ride Dangerous Lady in a thrilling Group race in the baking sunshine. She would triumph with her skilful tactics in the first downhill furlongs, and hold her lead to the line.

Crowds in the new grandstand would cheer The Lady. She would walk her proudly into the Winner's Enclosure to be greeted by a smiling Mike, with all the confidence of a new star.

It would be the beginning of her dazzling championship career.

But The Lady nipped her shoulder sharply, as sh

brushed her coat too hard in the small box at Arkenfield, dreaming of the future.

James Brant told Mr Mishima that, after all, he could not bear to part with Dangerous Lady.

Then he discovered that the obstacles had not disappeared. There were changes to his design-and-build tender. Loading bays were no longer needed, because the assembly-plant warehouse had switched to a 'just-in-time' system, which meant they would use fork-lift trucks instead.

Peter Cassell believed his story. Brant had casually mentioned that he had turned down half a million pounds, as if it were all his own.

But Nigel and Brian in Fenchurch Street were asking questions about his assets. They seemed to think that a valuation of Arkenfield would be helpful.

Jack Ross secretly despised flat racing. He belonged to the different world of the National Hunt. Jumping mighty steeplechase fences was the real sport. He had ridden in three Grand Nationals behind Red Rum and had followed the Irish mare Dawn Run over the hurdles at Cheltenham, a long way behind, on the day of her famous victory.

But the 'winter game' was dangerous. Jockeys broke bones regularly, tossed to the ground at between twenty-five and thirty miles an hour, once every dozen rides.

Many were forced to retire after serious injuries.

Jack was familiar with hospitals. He had broken his collar-bones several times, as well as his wrists, his ribs and his legs. Falls were part of the job, along with tiresome weeks of recovery.

It was not his shoulder or his split clavicle that worried him now. It was the persistent pain in his knees.

He stayed in hospital overnight, then ordered a taxi to take him home first thing in the morning, against the doctor's advice. With his arm held against his chest by the sling, he bent stiffly to pick up the post from the front door mat, relieved that Frances was not home yet.

Mike had not overslept for years. Frances tiptoed out of her room at eight o'clock, leaving him fast asleep.

She went downstairs and spoke to the Widow Ryan.

'Good morning, Miss Ross.'

'Good morning, Deirdre. Wonderful day.'

The sun shone into the hall through the open front doors.

'You had another message from Mr Brant.'

'Oh? When?'

'Very early. I didn't want to disturb you. It wasn't anything urgent.'

'What did he say?'

'You're to make your way back to England. Take your time, he said. No rush at all. Sounds a very nice man.'

Frances began to wonder if James Brant had a hand in the matchmaking. Her mind was confused.

'Thank you, Deirdre . . .'

Deirdre Ryan smiled, knowingly. She thought that they made a perfect young couple. Her own husband had looked a bit like Mike, too many years ago.

'Will Mr Hardy be down for his breakfast?'

'Oh, I expect he will.'

She walked through into the dining-room and found fresh roses on their table. She sat and stared at them, in a mist of speculation about how her life would change now, while a cheery waitress brought tea.

Rachael refused to buy James Brant's half of Dangerous Lady, even though he had reduced the price. He saved himself the humiliation of having to admit that he needed the money by blustering about his lack of control. They had reached an infuriating stalemate in the Arkenfield office.

John Grey detected the embattled look in James Brant's eyes, but he followed Rachael's reasoning. If the two-year-old filly were to be resold at public auction, so soon after her last change of ownership, the price would certainly be less than they paid. Buyers would be suspicious. James Brant would make a loss. She would pick up his share on the cheap.

So they reached an understanding.

The Lady would run at Goodwood, as planned. Mike and Frances would not be told about any of their schemes. Brant's secret would be kept, to prevent more disruption, and Joe's traitorous thoughts would be ignored.

Joe had agreed to that with relief.

Mike ate an enormous plate of bacon and eggs, with fried bread.

'Can't think why I overslept,' he said, innocently.

'Must be the air,' Frances suggested.

He had followed her down an hour later, and was not quite sure what to say. She told him about James Brant, expecting an outburst, but Mike did not seem to care. Arkenfield was then a long way off.

'There's a flight at ten past one,' she said, eventually. 'Think we could make it?'

'If we don't get lost again . . .'

She was heart-warmed to see that his eyes were smilin[g]

Jack Ross studied the envelopes, without opening the le[t]ters. He knew that the one addressed to him was from t[h]e Jockey Club and dreaded finding out what it said.

Another, from the United States, was for Frances.

The rest were bills and junk mail.

He finally tore the corner of his letter with his teet[h] and fingered it open with one hand.

It was just as he had feared.

Her Rover drew in to the yard in the afternoon, when [it] was still. Horses were dozing on their feet, in the shade [of] their boxes. The sun blazed outside.

The lads had gone to the Dog, with Joe. Only M[o] remained behind, doing her strenuous physical exercis[es] when no one was looking. She was getting ready for h[er] chance in the big race.

'What are we going to say?' Frances asked.

'To your dad, you mean?'

'To all of them . . . ?'

They sat in the car for a moment in silence. Wor[ds] seemed to be unnecessary. Mike kissed her, then he g[ot] out, taking his bag from the back seat.

'Don't worry. Leave it to me. See you later.'

Frances reversed into the lane outside and drove off.

Mike carried his bag across to the office and dump[ed] it. Then he spotted Mo, in a bathing suit, hiding in t[he] doorway of the round tack-room.

'Hey, what are you doing?'

'Training, Guv'nor. Hotter than a sauna in here. B[ut] don't come in. I've not got me clothes.'

Mike laughed.

'Training for what? Goodwood?'

He gathered from the slammed door that it was no laughing matter.

The Jockey Club letter said that the Stewards had to receive confirmation of Jack Ross's fitness from their own Medical Officer, before they would consider granting him a new licence.

Jack thought that he might be able to fool the orthopaedic surgeons in the local hospital. He was a master at concealing pain. But their man would find him out easily, because he knew that jockeys lied about their health.

His shoulder and collar-bone would soon mend.

But the legs were useless.

He heard Frances open the front door.

'Dad? I'm back. You all right?'

He would have to tell her the truth. He would have to find the courage to face it.

He would never ride again.

'We need a first-class pilot,' said James Brant, a few days later. 'I suggest someone like Steve Moorcroft.'

'Ronnie Foulkes, if he makes the weight – he'd do,' Joe put in.

They were all sitting in the Arkenfield office, planning the race at Goodwood the following week.

Through the grimy windows, they could see Dangerous Lady being made to stand in the yard.

Mo took opportunity to advertise herself, when she saw the cars arrive. Rachael's red Saab, Brant's white BMW, Frances' Rover, John Grey's beautiful old silver-blue Alvis, were all parked in the lane.

A good time to demonstrate her mastery. It had take
her hours of schooling to get the fractious filly to stand.

'What about Mouse?'

'No weight advantage. Allowances aren't claimable in
Group race. And her old man's riding Blitzkrieg for Hugo

'Paul Steele's definitely out,' said Joe, with feeling.

'We want a big name,' Brant insisted, 'Moorcroft's ou
man. Right at the top, even though he's how old?'

'Pushing forty, must be.'

'Forty-three,' said Mike, looking out, thoughtfully.

'Still up there with a chance of the championship. Wha
is he? Third?'

'Seventh. Look, I've got a suggestion . . .'

They all turned to Mike, who stood by the window.

Frances read the letter from the United States her fathe
had handed her when she came home from Ireland. Sh
was surprised to find it came from Darrell Woodfor
owner of the Fairlight Stud in Kentucky.

It had changed everything.

When she told Mike that she had been offered a jo
out of the blue, as an Assistant to her former employe
he had been careful in his reply.

'It would open a lot of doors, Frances.'

'Yes, I know.'

'You must've made a hell of an impression on him whe
you were there.'

'Wasn't aware of it. Bastard to work for. Drives sta
into the ground.'

'This is why the Fairlight is the biggest and best i
Kentucky.'

'Probably, yes . . .'

They had sat in the evening sun, beside the ancient brooding stones of the Long Barrow, high on The Rudge. 'What about your Dad?'

'Well, he says he wants me to go.'

Mike had said nothing to dissuade her. They had walked slowly back to the Discovery in the twilight, as dusk fell over the Downs, and had not mentioned it since.

There were immediate protests against Mike's suggestion.

'Mo Ratcliffe? Just an apprentice! Can't take stupid risks like that!' James Brant stated, flatly.

Mike was not deterred.

'She knows The Lady better than anyone. They're a team, those two. She can ride. Best young horsewoman I've seen. Worked hard for it. Done everything right. And straight sprint over six furlongs – all it needs is a good break out of the stalls.'

'Sticking your neck out a mile, Mike,' said Frances. 'But if you really think so, then I'll go along . . .'

John Grey was adamant.

'A good horse needs a good jockey. Get Stevie Moorcroft, if you can. He may not win, but he won't lose it.'

'Rachael?'

'I'm on the fence. But I want The Lady to have the best chance of winning this race, for all our sakes.'

'Joe? You've seen her. What's your opinion?'

Joe Hogan felt awkward, as James Brant glared at him. He saw John Grey's set face. Rachael twisted her hands.

'Up to you, Guv'nor . . .'

James Brant would not let him get away with that.

'Come on, Joe. You're a blasted shareholder. Your money as well. Do you want Mo Ratcliffe to get the ride or not?'

All their eyes were on him.

Even Rosie the Dragon, who was back at work, waited for his reply.

Joe looked out of the window at the girl in the yard. He had grown quite fond of her over the months. He knew that she would succeed one day.

He shook his head, sadly.

Mo was not there for evening stables.

Joe told Nick and Danny to do her two, ready for Mike's inspection. The Lady bit Danny's arm when he was dressing her over in the box. He took a short, thick wooden stick and smacked her quarters.

Later, they realized that Mo had gone. Her small room in the Hilton was left unlocked. The old second-hand wardrobe was empty and her few belongings had been cleared out of the chest of drawers. Posters of her racing heroes had been taken down from the walls.

A big colour photograph of Steve Moorcroft, in his Championship year, lay ripped in two on her bed.

Mike had tried to be tactful, knowing that Mo was head-strong. He wanted to tell her that he had been prepared to give her the ride. It was unusual for a trainer to stand up for a girl jockey, especially one as inexperienced as Mo, but he felt it was right.

But she had not stayed to listen.

She ran off to her room as soon as he mentioned Steve Moorcroft, and he thought it was wise to leave her alone.

Her motor bike roared out of the yard in the afternoon, but he paid no attention. She would have to learn to accept that his decision was final.

Frances did not know what to do.

She had telephoned Darrell Woodford to explain that her father had taken another fall.

She could not leave him alone with his arm in a sling.

But she knew that it was an excuse, to put off reaching a decision. Her father managed perfectly well with one hand. He had lots of practice at dealing with injuries.

Darrell Woodford was most sympathetic, but he needed to know soon. He told her more about the job, in his familiar drawl.

She had not realized how old he was.

In a year or two, he intended to retire. He wanted an Assistant to train in the management of the stud, with that very much in mind.

It was too good an opportunity to miss.

Her father had told her that his riding days were over.

'And that's official. No come back. No riding out, even.'

'Oh, Dad . . .'

'So I've been thinking. Doing a bit at Arkenfield, while you were in Ireland, I got the taste.'

'For what?'

'Training. Nothing grand, a few jumpers to start with . . .'

She had laughed. He was impossible.

Then she thought about Mike. If she was in love with him, how could she think of leaving to go to America?

Mo rode her motor bike, with its packed panniers, steadily north up the A34 to Oxford. She followed signs automatically, on through Chipping Norton to Stratford-upon-Avon.

She stopped by the river and trudged along the embankment, looking at swans drifting by. Tourists in twos and threes crowded over the bridge, dressed in light summer clothes, talking.

None of them would understand.

Then she continued blindly north, on the same road, stopping at garages for fuel and bars of chocolate, with no idea where she was going.

Soon, she was lost in the sprawling outskirts of Birmingham.

In the office, Mike tried to concentrate. The County Stakes was an important race for two-year-olds. A precursor to the Classics of the following season. Winners of the Stakes often went on to run in the Guineas.

Steve Moorcroft had two other rides at Goodwood on the same day, so he was quite willing to accept a third.

Mike wanted him to work The Lady first on the gallops, but that was harder to organize.

Top jockeys were busy men, working a sixteen-hour day in the season, often attending more than one meeting, sometimes hundreds of miles apart, driving between them, or flying in private light aircraft.

Mo had won well on Raw Silk, claiming her 7lb apprentice allowance. She would lose that advantage in a Group race, of course, but Mike was sure she could win the Stakes.

Now she had disappeared and The Lady was unsettled. He wished that the others had agreed to his suggestion.

James Brant invited Peter Cassell and his wife to Goodwood. Nigel and Brian said that they may tag along, just for the day out. All of them wanted to meet the famous Steve Moorcroft.

Secretly, they were impressed.

*

Rachael arranged to go with John Grey in his car. She would bring a picnic hamper, with food and white wine. If it was sunny, she planned to wear a smart summer dress, and a straw hat with a big blue bow.

Steve Moorcroft's sleek red XJS Jaguar arrived at Arkenfield two days before the race.

Mike admired his fluid riding style on the gallops. Nick and Danny watched enviously, as the professional made it look easy. Dangerous Lady behaved herself impeccably for him, why not for them?

Mo threaded her way through the Birmingham traffic. She was swept along by the tide heading north.

A couple of hours later, numbed and exhausted, she swung into a tree-lined road in the Greater Manchester suburb of Wythenshawe.

She stopped outside a small, semi-detached council house, and rang the two-tone chimes.

It was a long time before her mother answered the door.

Mike had tried to tidy his squalid rooms over the office, but they looked a mess when he led Frances upstairs the next night. Paper peeled from the damp walls. The threadbare carpets were stained.

He did not want to leave the yard unattended. Joe and the lads had gone to the Dog, so he stayed behind, concerned about security.

Nothing must go wrong before the Goodwood meeting, due to start the following afternoon.

Frances peered into the cramped, poorly equipped kitchen with a sniff of distaste. Unwashed dishes were stacked in the sink.

'Have you said anything to your dad yet?' Mike called out, shifting piles of old newspapers from the sofa.

'I really haven't decided whether to go or not,' she replied, hesitantly.

'I meant about us . . .'

A faint shadow had passed between them. The first thing on her mind had been the job in Kentucky, not him.

'Oh, Mike, what shall I do?'

Frances suddenly rushed into his arms. Mike drew her close and kissed her, but he could almost feel her slipping away from him . . .

Hot late-July sun blazed over glorious Goodwood.

Festive crowds swarmed in the stands and spread far over the bright green parkland, happy to be at the races.

White-coated attendants showed little patience with free spirits and forced all the drivers of vehicles into tidy lanes.

Mike backed the silver Arkenfield Land-Rover Discovery into a slot in the Owners' and Trainers' sector, and ran towards the stables, leaving Frances to assist her father on his slow walk to the stands.

Flags flew over the hospitality tents and the commentator addressed the crowds,

'Good afternoon, ladies and gentlemen. We look forward to an exciting day here at Goodwood. We have six important races for you . . .'

Jockey Club officials strode about the Weighing Room dressed in uniformly well-cut suits, looking as if they shared the same Savile Row tailor, speaking sharply on portable telephones.

The Clerk of the Scales sat at his desk, as a line of multicoloured jockeys waited to be weighed out in front of him. One after another, they laid their silk caps down and sat on the big machine, displaying their number cloths.

'Number seven, sir. No extras.'

'You are S. Moorcroft?' asked the Clerk, checking his colours against the racecard.

'Yes, sir.'

'Red, yellow circle, right. Carrying eight stone. You're a bit light. Another pound, I think.'

The Clerk selected a sliver of lead and flipped it across to the jockey, who slipped it into his weight-cloth.

The Judge climbed up to his eyrie, the Stewards took their places, and the Starter set off to the start.

Moorcroft checked the girth on Dangerous Lady as the bell rang for the jockeys to mount.

Mike curtly gave his instructions.

'Hands and heels. Don't get boxed. Bring her home in one piece. See you in the Winner's Enclosure.'

He legged him into the plate. Danny and Joe led the resplendent bay filly down to the course gates, where they released her to canter off in the front of the packed stands.

The PA commentator announced each of the runners as they appeared, in racecard order.

'And next we have the clear favourite for the Group 3 County Stakes, with a prize to the winner of £50,000, it's number seven, Dangerous Lady, ridden by Stevie Moorcroft. She's followed by the grey colt Blitzkrieg, the mount of Ronnie Foulkes . . .'

There were ten runners for the six-furlong sprint.

James Brant poured champagne in his high private box, with a splendid panoramic view over The Clump to the high Downs on the horizon. Kath, under his strict orders, did her best to entertain the wives of the guests. Brant dismissed the prize as unimportant, but dropped hints about the large amounts of money he expected to make from Classic wins, in The Lady's three-year-old career.

Peter Cassell tried to explain the staggering economics to Nigel and Brian, who sipped champagne and tasted the bland canapés. But apart from raising an occasional eyebrow, they appeared to be not very interested.

'Of course, it isn't the money,' said Brant, expansively, 'it's the thrill of seeing her win . . .'

Rachael looked demure under her wide-brimmed straw hat. She and John Grey had lunched on smoked salmon sandwiches, with chilled Chablis she had stored in an iced cooling-box. They strolled in the sunshine eating strawberries and cream, until the County Stakes runners were circling behind the starting stalls. Then they made their way to the stands, to join Mike, Jack and Frances.

Dangerous Lady refused to enter the stalls at first, so the handlers led her in hooded, encouraged by a rope quoit held behind her.

The commentator began his litany in a flat monotone, 'Under Starter's Orders . . . and they're off.'

Joe Hogan stood at the rails, in his usual spot by the gates. He suddenly noticed a familiar figure, crouched near the winning post. He was sure that it was Mo Ratcliffe.

'Hey, Mo!' he shouted, but she didn't hear him over the expectant buzz of the crowds.

She had stayed with her mother for two nights.

The irritating words, 'Oh, fancy!' were all that she heard

when she described her career at Arkenfield, and her win on Raw Silk.

A big-bellied lorry driver, who shared her mother's bed, came back on the second night from a long-distance haul, and Mo left first thing the next morning.

She rode her motor bike south towards the only home she knew, and the splendid four-legged creature only she understood.

The break from the stalls was all-important. Dangerous Lady burst out from a high draw position, with a good chance.

In short races, tactics were vital. They could be won or lost in the first furlong.

The straight course at Goodwood starts with a rise, descends for three furlongs, then flattens out, with a rise again at the finish.

She was boxed in behind the leaders, who crossed over and bunched up ahead of her during the first uphill stretch.

Moorcroft pulled wide to pass them, but he lost precious ground.

The Lady's astonishing speed showed on the downward slope. She soon brought the field back to her. By the halfway pole, there were only three in front.

The commentator's voice boomed over the wildly yelling spectators,

'Dangerous Lady's making her run on the far side, but it's still Blitzkrieg the leader, being pressed hard by Little Saki on the stand side, then Rose Felicia ... Dangerous Lady, living up to her name, as they enter the final furlong ... Dangerous Lady in second place now as they race for the line, it's still Blitzkrieg in front ...'

Ronnie Foulkes flashed his whip to urge the powerful grey along.

Mo grasped the rail and leaped up and down, shouting, 'Come on, Lady! You can do it!'

James Brant bellowed frantic, raucous encouragement from the box, his eyes fastened to binoculars.

Frances waved her straw hat in the air, and John Grey applauded.

The Lady continued to gain as they neared the line. She drew almost level with the big, majestically striding grey. The crowds went wild with excitement at the breathtaking finish.

Mike clenched his teeth and silently willed her to make a last desperate lung-bursting effort . . .

But Hugo Latimer's Blitzkrieg, whipped on by Ronnie Foulkes, passed the post first by a neck.

Disappointment clouded all of them, as if the sun had gone in. The bright day ended with an overwhelming sense of loss.

A sense of the awful possibility of failure gripped James Brant, as Nigel and Brian looked at him with pale sympathy. They were not foolish enough to waste their money on horses.

Peter Cassell was satisfied that he had showed good sense in buying a cheap hunter for his wife, instead of an expensive thoroughbred. It confirmed his long-held opinion about the folly of risk-taking.

Kath touched her husband's arm with tenderness. She was still proud of what he was.

Joe Hogan and Danny caught The Lady's reins and led her steaming and blowing towards the Winner's Enclosure, where she occupied the number two stall.

Mike stood on the steps of the Weighing Room, with a desolate look on his face, as Steve Moorcroft slid nimbly down from the saddle.

He did not trust himself to say anything to the jockey.

David Ware and Hugo Latimer smiled, as they prepared to receive the prize.

Mo Ratcliffe escaped from Goodwood immediately after the race, concealing her face in her motor bike helmet. She rode all afternoon through the quiet country lanes, trying to control her disappointment. She knew that if she had ridden The Lady, they would have won.

By evening, she was high on The Rudge, well off the road, trying to find courage under a vast cloudless sky.

Mike stood in the lane by the hedge, looking up at the weather-vane shaped like a galloping racehorse, black against the heavens.

Frances held his hand, tightly.

All the inquisitions after the race had established nothing. Steve Moorcroft's other two rides were successful for him. He frankly admitted to running the wrong race on Dangerous Lady.

But Mike did not believe him.

He thought he knew the reason for Dangerous Lady's defeat, and he wished he had followed his first instinct. Instincts would make him, or break him.

'Given Darrell Woodford your answer yet?' he asked.

'No, but I will tomorrow.'

'Next season, Arkenfield will take up every minute of my time..'

'Are you trying to say there's no room in your life for me?'

'I'm saying I know how important that job is to you. If you stay here, just because of us, somewhere along the line it will rebound.'

She moved closer to him.

Mike kissed her, and then said,

'My feelings won't change — whether you're in the States, or anywhere else.'

'Neither will mine,' she whispered.

They both realized the implication behind her words . . .

As they walked slowly back to the gates of Arkenfield in the gathering dusk, they heard a motor bike approaching.

The single eye of its headlamp lit the wooden board, as it swung into the yard ahead of them.

They could clearly see the painted letters:

ARKENFIELD STABLES
Trainer: Michael Hardy
Arkenfield, Berkshire

Twelve thousand miles away, in the Australian winter, a small boy called Tom posted a parcel containing coloured crayon drawings of horses, to his father in England.

All Pan books are available at your local bookshop or newsagent, or can be ordered direct from the publisher. Indicate the number of copies required and fill in the form below.

Send to: **CS Department, Pan Books Ltd., P.O. Box 40, Basingstoke, Hants. RG21 2YT.**

or phone: 0256 469551 (Ansaphone), quoting title, author and Credit Card number.

Please enclose a remittance* to the value of the cover price plus: 60p for the first book plus 30p per copy for each additional book ordered to a maximum charge of £2.40 to cover postage and packing.

*Payment may be made in sterling by UK personal cheque, postal order, sterling draft or international money order, made payable to Pan Books Ltd.

Alternatively by Barclaycard/Access:

Card No.

Signature:

Applicable only in the UK and Republic of Ireland.

While every effort is made to keep prices low, it is sometimes necessary to increase prices at short notice. Pan Books reserve the right to show on covers and charge new retail prices which may differ from those advertised in the text or elsewhere.

NAME AND ADDRESS IN BLOCK LETTERS PLEASE:

....

Name ————————————————————————

Address ————————————————————————

————————————————————————

————————————————————————

————————————————————————

3/87